04/19

P9-DDB-790

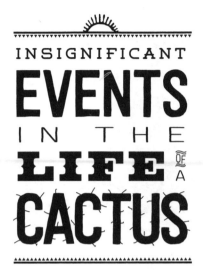

INSIGNIFICANT

EVENTS

IN THE

LIFE OF A

CACTUS

INSIGNIFICANT EVENTS IN THE LIFE OF A CACTUS

DUSTI BOWLING

STERLING CHILDREN'S BOOKS
New York

STERLING CHILDREN'S BOOKS
New York

An Imprint of Sterling Publishing Co., Inc.
1166 Avenue of the Americas
New York, NY 10036

ISBN 978-1-4549-2345-9

Library of Congress Cataloging-in-Publication Data

Names: Bowling, Dusti, author.
Title: Insignificant events in the life of a cactus / by Dusti Bowling.
Description: New York : Sterling Children's Books, [2017] | Summary: New
   friends and a mystery help Aden, thirteen, adjust to middle school and
   life at a dying western theme park in a new state, where her being born
   armless presents many challenges.
Identifiers: LCCN 2017021165 | ISBN 9781454923459 (hardback)
Subjects: | CYAC: People with disabilities--Fiction. | Amusement
   parks--Fiction. | Friendship--Fiction. | Adoption--Fiction. | Tourette
   syndrome--Fiction. | Overweight persons--Fiction. | Moving,
   Household--Fiction. | Mystery and detective stories. | BISAC: JUVENILE
   FICTION / Social Issues / Special Needs. | JUVENILE FICTION / Social
   Issues / Friendship. | JUVENILE FICTION / Family / Adoption.
Classification: LCC PZ7.1.B6872 Ins 2017 | DDC [Fic]--dc23 LC record available at
   https://lccn.loc.gov/2017021165

Distributed in Canada by Sterling Publishing Co., Inc.
c/o Canadian Manda Group, 664 Annette Street
Toronto, Ontario, M6S 2C8, Canada
Distributed in the United Kingdom by GMC Distribution Services
Castle Place, 166 High Street, Lewes, East Sussex, BN7 1XU, England
Distributed in Australia by NewSouth Books
45 Beach Street, Coogee, NSW 2034, Australia

For information about custom editions, special sales, and premium and corporate purchases,
please contact Sterling Special Sales at 800-805-5489 or specialsales@sterlingpublishing.com.

Manufactured in the United States of America

Lot #:
6 8 10 9 7 5
08/18

sterlingpublishing.com

Design by Ryan Thomann
Case cover art: © valik/iStockphoto
Endpaper art: © pie-guy/iStockphoto
Title page art: iStockphoto: © aklionka (plants); © wissanu99 (cacti)
Author photo by Zachary Bowling

FOR BRONTE

YOU CAN DO ANYTHING

WHEN I WAS LITTLE, A KID POINTED

at me on the playground and shouted, "Her arms fell off!" then ran away screaming in terror to his mom, who had to cuddle him on her lap and rub his head for like ten minutes to get him to calm down. I think, up until then, I hadn't thought about the idea that my arms must have *actually* fallen off at some point in my life. I had never really thought about not having arms at all.

My missing arms weren't an issue for me or my parents. I never once heard either of them say, "Oh, no, Aven can't possibly do that because that's only for armed people," or "Poor Aven is so helpless without arms," or "Maybe Aven can do that one day, you know, if she ever grows some arms." They always said things like, "You'll have to do this differently from other people, but you can manage," and "I know this is challenging. Keep trying," and "You're capable of anything, Aven."

I had never realized just how different I was until the day that horrible kid shouted about my arms having fallen off. For the first time I found myself aware of my total armlessness, and I guess I felt like I was sort of naked all of a sudden. So I, too, ran to my mom, and she scooped me up and carried me away from the park, allowing my tears and snot to soak her shirt.

As she drove us home that day, I sat whimpering in my car seat and asked her what had happened to my arms and why they'd fallen off. She told me they hadn't fallen off; I was just born like that. I asked her how I could get some new ones. She said I couldn't. I wailed in despair, and she told me to stop crying because having arms was totally overrated. I didn't know what *overrated* meant at the time because, like I said, I was really little and so was my brain. I kind of figured it out over the next few days, though, because my parents were constantly saying things like, "Coloring this picture with my hands is okay, but if only I could color it with my feet like Aven. Now that would be fantastic," and "Eating spaghetti with my arms is just so boring. I wish I could eat it with my feet," and "The only person I know who can pick their nose with their toes is Aven. She sure is a special little girl." Dad even went so far as to ask Mom if there were any arm-removal services in the area.

Growing up, I could do most everything everyone else with arms could do: eating cereal, brushing my teeth and hair, getting dressed, and yes, even wiping my own bottom. I know you're instantly wondering how I do it, and maybe I'll tell you later . . . maybe. Until then, you'll just have to live in suspense.

Sure, these things take longer for me. Sometimes they take *a lot* longer. Sometimes I have to use a special tool like a hook or a strap or something like that. And every now and then I want to scream in frustration and kick a pillow until the stuffing comes out because it's taken me twenty minutes to get my pants buttoned. But I *can* button my pants.

I think I can do all these things because my parents have always encouraged me to figure things out on my own—well, more like *made* me figure things out on my own. I suppose if they had always done everything for me, I would be helpless without them. But they didn't, and I'm not. And now that I'm

thirteen years old, I don't need much help with anything. True story.

When I started kindergarten, the kids were a little weirded out by my lack of armage. I got asked just
about every day what had happened to my arms, as
well as a billion other silly questions—like how do I
make farting noises with my armpits when I don't
have arms or hands . . . or pits. And how do I play
dress-up—which I tried showing them and ended up
with a poofy pink tutu thing stuck around my head for
about five minutes before the teacher finally noticed
and helped me pull it down to my waist.

I got so tired of telling them the same boring story
about being born without arms that I started making
stuff up. It was stinking hilarious. I knew from the first
moment I told a girl my arms had burned off in a fire, I
had found a great hobby: making up stories. I loved the
way her eyes grew wide with shock and the way her voice
went all high-pitched with excitement as she asked me a
bunch more questions about my charred arms.

Her: "What kind of fire accident?"

Me: "A wild forest fire burning out of control!"

Her: "Where?"

Me: "In the mountains of Tanzania." (I honestly
didn't know where Tanzania was or if it had any

mountains. I think I had heard the name in an episode of *Scooby-Doo* or something.)

Her: "How old were you?"

Me: "Just a helpless baby. My mom barely rescued me in time. She pulled me from my burning crib and raced out of our flaming village, leaving a trail of fire all the way down the mountain as my arms burned to a crisp! They looked like two pieces of bacon by the time we got to the village hospital!"

Another kid standing nearby: "Cooked or uncooked?"

So I kind of traumatized her and had to have a meeting with my parents and the teacher later about my story. My parents squinted their eyes and pursed their lips and nodded their heads as the teacher told them, "Um, Aven told another child that her arms burned off in a wildfire in the mountains of Tanzania." She peered at them over her glasses, frowning. "She also mentioned something about bacon."

I had never seen such serious looks on my parents' faces before, like they were concentrating so hard on being serious, their heads might explode if they blinked. They said seriously they would talk to me about it and shook the teacher's hand seriously and gave me serious looks as we walked seriously out of school. But I could tell they weren't mad because all the way home one of them would softly snort and then the other would giggle and then the other would shake from laughing but trying not to laugh out loud and on and on like that all the way home.

They later told me just to be truthful so I didn't upset any other kids. And I did for a long time. But then one day in fifth grade, we had a new kid come to our school. (I had gone to the same school since kindergarten, so all my friends knew I was just born with no arms.) When I sat down at lunch with this kid, he said, "Whoa! What happened to your arms?"

All my friends were looking at me, and what can I say? It exploded out of me like an overfilled water balloon. I told him this crazy story about how I had rescued a puppy that had been tied to the train tracks just in time before a train nearly ran over it—just in time for the puppy . . . but not for my poor, flattened arms.

You should have seen the look on this kid's face—priceless. My best friend, Emily, burst out laughing and my friend Kayla spit chocolate milk across the table. The new kid realized it was a joke and started laughing, too.

Pretty soon everyone was constantly asking me, "Hey, Aven! Where'd your arms go?" And I would have a new story to tell. Over time my stories got more and more ridiculous: alligator wrestling in the Everglades in Florida, freak roller coaster accidents, skydiving trips gone wrong. I made my stories as ridiculous as possible so people would always know I was joking.

I grew up with those kids. I never felt out of place or anything like that. My armlessness wasn't strange or weird to them because, like I said, I had always gone to the same school.

I never imagined my parents would make me leave. I never thought they would make me move all the way to Arizona and go to a new school right after starting eighth grade.

Then again, I never imagined I would save the Old West, perform for an audience in the desert, and solve a mystery. You'd be surprised at all I'm capable of, though. Even without arms.

THE DAY DAD TOLD ME HE WANTED

to apply for a job as a theme park manager in Arizona, I thought it was quite possible aliens had taken over his brain—either aliens or the government. I knew from my great-grandma the government was capable of dreadful things. She was always saying stuff like, "If the public only knew what the government was up to, there would be a revolution!" and pumping her spotted, wrinkled fist in the air. I wasn't completely sure why an eighty-six-year-old woman who lived in a trailer in Kansas was the only person privy to this top-secret information, but she *clearly* was. So I wouldn't put it past the government to insert some kind of mind-control chip into Dad's brain and force him to run a crumbling theme park in the desert.

My parents discussed it with me one night over a dinner of buttered noodles, my favorite meal. Oh, man—I just realized they deliberately buttered me up with buttered noodles.

"So I got an email from a guy by the name of Joe Cavanaugh," Dad said over his noodles. "He owns a place called Stagecoach Pass."

"What's that?" I asked, slurping up a noodle.

"It's this western-themed amusement park in Arizona. I guess he found my résumé on one of the job sites where I posted it. Anyway, he invited me to apply for the position of general manager at the park."

"He must have been impressed with your résumé, Mister-Big-Time-Restaurant-Manager," said Mom.

"Well," said Dad, "I'm not really sure how managing a restaurant relates to managing an entire theme park, but I guess a huge part of their business is this steakhouse there, so that's probably why he contacted me."

"Are you going to apply?" I asked.

"It does sound interesting," said Dad.

I scowled. "Arizona is really far away."

"Don't forget you were born there, Sheebs," Dad said. "We spent a lot of time there during your adoption, and we really liked it. We even thought it might be a great place to retire one day. The winter was so beautiful—warm and sunny. I'm sick of icy winters."

"What's the summer like?" I asked.

Mom grimaced. "I've heard it's kind of like the surface of the sun."

"It could be an exciting adventure." Dad waggled his eyebrows at me. "Swimming and soccer all year long."

I glared at my noodles. "I don't think I want to play soccer on the surface of the sun."

"Come on," said Dad. "You're such a pro, you could play soccer anywhere."

"Stop trying to entice me," I said. "You haven't even applied yet."

"Well, if it's okay with you, I'd like to."

On the one hand, the thought of leaving Kansas, and the only home I could ever remember, sounded worse than anything. On the other, Dad had lost his job nearly six months earlier, when the restaurant he'd been managing went out of business. He really needed this.

"It's okay with me," I mumbled, feeling like I might cry.

Dad applied. And then he and Mom were invited to go to Arizona for an interview and to check the place out. And then they were invited to stay and run the theme park together. Turns out it was more of a two-person job.

And so we sold off a ton of our furniture and donated the junk we didn't need and packed the rest of our belongings into a giant pod that would magically disappear from Kansas and magically reappear in Arizona a week later. We drove our old car over a thousand miles westward across the country, praying the entire time we wouldn't break down.

We managed to make it in one single long day without stopping at a hotel until we got to Phoenix. By the time we arrived, Dad's eyes looked like Atomic Fireballs and Mom's hair looked like she'd taken a spin in a hairspray cyclone.

Early the next morning, we drove by the giant covered wagon with **STAGECOACH PASS** printed on it in large brown block letters, and I saw the park for the first time.

Then I knew for sure the government and mind-control chips were involved.

WE PARKED IN THE LARGE DIRT
parking lot and got out of the car. I squinted from
the bright, hot sun. Had the sun been this bright in
Kansas? I didn't think so.

I looked around. I'd never seen so much brown
before—not a patch of grass anywhere. Did grass even
exist in Arizona? Again, I didn't think so.

We walked over the compacted dirt toward the
entrance, which wasn't closed up, even though the park
wasn't open yet—I guess they weren't too worried
about people sneaking in. A lizard skittered across the
dirt in front of me, and I jumped back.

The dirt. Never. Ended. There were no sidewalks or
grass or paved anything at Stagecoach Pass—just dirt
and old wooden buildings with old wooden steps and

old wooden porches that looked like they might collapse at any time.

"Good morning!" a cheerful, gray-mustached man greeted us from one of these porches. He wore a cowboy hat and held a mug of something steamy. Coffee? In this heat?

"Good morning," Mom and Dad said at the same time.

"Nice to see you again, Gary," said Mom. I looked at her. "He's the one who interviewed us," she whispered to me. "He's the accountant for the park."

Gary walked down the steps. "And this must be Aven."

"Our one and only," Dad said, squeezing his arm around me.

I gave Gary a polite smile. He seemed nice enough, even though his gray mustache was awfully pointy.

"Well," Gary said, tossing his coffee on the dirt, where it dried in about two seconds, "I bet you're tired after your long trip. I'll take you up to the apartment."

As we trudged toward our new living quarters, which were apparently located right over the steakhouse, Dad asked, "So when do we get to meet Joe Cavanaugh?"

"Oh, no one ever meets Joe," said Gary. "Not around here much."

"That's strange," said Mom. "A business owner who doesn't visit his own business?"

Gary smiled and tilted his hat at her. "That's why Joe needs good managers, ma'am."

Mom and Dad had described the apartment as a cozy but humble little place. They weren't kidding about the cozy. Or the humble. Or the little.

Gary and a few other men from the park (all dressed like cowboys), carried our stuff up from the car. After Mom and I finished putting away my suitcase of bare necessities, she said to me, "Why don't you go out and explore, honey?"

"What's there to explore?"

"Tons of stuff," she said. "There's a gold mine, and a gift shop, and a museum, and a soda shop. You could get yourself an ice cream." She looked at her watch. "It won't be open for a half hour, though."

So I went out and explored. For about five minutes. The heat got more and more intense with every second until I was forced into the air-conditioned museum.

The museum was actually more like a room—just one room with picture-covered walls and a few "artifacts" in glass cases. These artifacts included a collection of stone arrowheads, some broken Navajo pottery pieces, a pistol from the 1800s, a pair of old spurs, and a genuine dead tarantula with an information board that shared facts like, tarantulas have no teeth, so they use their venom to liquefy their prey and suck up the liquid nastiness directly into their stomachs. How awesome is that?

I scanned the framed photographs on the walls, the old wooden floorboards creaking under my feet. Most of the pictures were black and white, taken a long time ago when Stagecoach Pass first opened. It looked like it was quite the place back then—crowds and rodeos and even parades on Main Street. Then I came to an empty space on the wall, where it seemed a picture had been removed. The nameplate beneath the empty space had been left up and said *The Cavanaughs, Stagecoach Pass, 2004.*

I looked around at the rest of the photos and each of their nameplates, but I couldn't find any more of the Cavanaughs. I thought about what Gary had said: *No one ever meets Joe.* And I wondered why.

"There you are," Dad said from behind me. "I've been looking for you."

I turned around. "Just getting some cool air."

"Don't worry." Dad wiped the sweat from his forehead. "It will cool down soon. Guess what?"

"What?"

"The rodeo arena is all closed down, so I thought we could set up a soccer goal out there and practice."

"That sounds great."

"You want to go kick the ball around now?"

"Isn't it too hot?"

"Never. Plus, we can keep cool with ice cream."

"What if I get a sunburn?"

"They have sunblock in the gift shop."

I smiled. "You have an answer for everything, don't you?"

Dad put an arm around me and led me into the gift shop. "Of course. Didn't you know that dads know everything?"

I snorted as he picked out a small tube of sunblock from a rack. "I'd like to be there when you tell Mom that."

EVEN THOUGH THE NEW SCHOOL

year had already started, my parents gave me a couple of days to settle in before sending me off to be tortured.

Desert Ridge Middle School was only a few miles from Stagecoach Pass, and Mom drove me my first day. I sat in my seat, staring straight ahead, my heart pounding. When we turned into the parking lot of my new giant school, I thought my heart might just pound right out of my chest. My school back in Kansas only had about three hundred students. Desert Ridge was more than three times that size—a thousand kids who had never seen me before.

Mom drove our old clunker up to the drop-off curb behind a bunch of other cars—mostly fancy cars like BMWs, Volvos, and Jeeps, all shiny and freshly waxed in a variety of bright colors. Our can't-tell-what-the-color-is car didn't even have a logo because it had fallen off a long time ago. Actually, I'm not sure my parents remembered what kind of car it was. It definitely didn't fit in with the other cars, and I took that as a bad sign. We waited as the line inched forward.

Mom turned to me. Her lips twitched a bit as she smiled. "You want me to walk you in?"

I shook my head. "No."

She nodded and pushed a long strand of dark hair behind her ear. "Yeah, I suppose that would be embarrassing—having your mommy walk you in on your first day."

"Just a little."

She ran her hand down my hair and tugged lightly on the tips. "You remember where your first class is?"

"Yep. No problem."

"You remember where your locker is?"

"All systems go . . . in my brain," I said as we pulled up right in front of the curb.

"Oh, good," she said, "because I was a little bit worried this morning when you came out with your shirt on backward and then stuck your cereal in the microwave."

"Just being an airhead." I slid my head under the

strap of my bag. That wasn't exactly the truth. I was nervous. *Extremely* nervous.

"I know how hard things have been for you, sweet-heart," she said.

"I'm fine, Mom. Really . . . I'll be okay today."

She leaned over and kissed the top of my head. "Call if you need anything. I'll pick you up right out here after school."

Normally my parents never baby me. They're more the kind of parents who, instead of kissing your boo-boos, tell you to walk it off and be a man. And they never have seemed to care that I'm not actually a man. But I guess today was a special occasion. Honestly, I wished she would stop—it was stressing me out even more.

I nodded and opened the car door with my foot, then slid it back into my new purple ballet flat. I got out of the car, swung my bag around to my side, gave Mom a reassuring smile, and slammed the door shut with my hip.

Before I'd walked five steps, I got my first *look*. I tried to ignore it. My parents had always taught me to tackle one small goal at a time—holding a brush between my toes, lifting that brush all the way to my head, running the brush through my hair. One small goal at a time. And so I zeroed in on my first goal of the day—getting to my first class without barfing up all my soggy, microwaved cereal.

We had visited the school yesterday so I could find my classes, meet some of my teachers, and talk with the people in the office. Everyone was super nice and caring, of course, but they all said the same thing so much, it started to get annoying: "If there's anything you need, Aven, don't be afraid to ask." Like they just knew I was going to need a lot of extra help.

I speed-walked to the science room, not just to avoid the other kids' stares, but also because it was so stinking hot. By the time I got to my class, sweat was already trickling down my forehead. I went straight to my seat, swung my school bag onto my desk, and slid the strap off over my head. I eased my foot out of my flat, opened the top of my bag with it, and pulled out my science book.

One benefit of living in Arizona was that I could wear ballet flats (my favorite kind of shoe) year-round—not at all like in Kansas, where I had to wear warm boots in the winter. Everything took longer when I wore warm boots. It was so much easier to slip my foot in and out of flats. I had pairs in brown, black, rainbow stripes, flowers, and now purple. Flip-flops probably would

have been even easier, but there's the whole dust fac-
tor. And it's especially dusty in the desert.

I glanced up and found Ms. Hart, the science
teacher, watching me. I smiled a little and she smiled
back. I had met her last night, and she had told me to
let her know if I needed any help, of course. I hoped
she could see now that I didn't need extra help as I
proceeded to pull a notebook and pencil out of my bag
with my foot.

I took my seat and turned to the girl sitting next to
me. The girl's eyes widened in obvious surprise. "Are . . .
are you new?" she asked.

"Yes," I replied. "It's my first day." It stunk to be
starting eighth grade over a month into the school year.

I could tell the girl was desperately trying not to
look at my nonexistent arms. People were *always* doing
that—like if they looked down at my torso for longer
than a split second, they would turn to stone. Like my
torso was actually Medusa's head.

The girl was pretty, with her long dark hair and
strappy red dress and all her body parts. I always
wanted to wear a dress with skinny straps like that, but
I guess I felt too self-conscious about it; the strappy
dress wouldn't look the same without some nice long
arms to show off in it.

"Well, welcome." She quickly pulled out her books and started reading, surely to avoid having to talk to me anymore.

I turned my attention to my own book and then looked back at the girl. "What page are we on?" I asked her.

"Twenty-three." She reached for my book. "Here, I'll help—"

"Oh no, that's okay," I said. She stopped and pulled her hand away. I lifted my foot and opened the book with it, using my dexterous toes to turn the pages until I got to page twenty-three. "See? I can do it."

She gave me a twitchy smile. "How'd you learn to do that?"

I shrugged. "You'd be surprised what you can do with your feet when that's all you have."

She gave me another uncomfortable smile and went back to reading her book. She hadn't introduced herself, so I didn't either. I sometimes wondered if people had a tendency not to give me their names or ask me for mine because of their fear of getting too close . . . too close to something so different.

At lunchtime I decided to sit outside on a bench to eat. I didn't want to go to the cafeteria and sit at a table by myself while everyone watched me eat with my feet; I might as well have been up on a stage with a spotlight shining on me. I pulled my lunch out of my bag, but then I noticed a few kids standing around glancing at me. I knew what they were doing—waiting to watch me eat. Everyone was always curious.

At home in Kansas, I'd have been sitting at a table with Emily, Kayla, and Brittney, all of us laughing about the booger hanging out of Mr. Thompson's hairy nose during history class. Kayla would be tossing pretzels at me while I tried to catch them in my mouth, and Emily would be complaining that her parents still wouldn't let her wear makeup. No one would have cared that I was eating with my feet.

My stomach cramped. I stuck my lunch back in my school bag and headed for the bathroom, where I was grateful to find automatic water and soap dispensers. In my nervousness I had forgotten to wash my feet, which I always do before I eat (just because I don't have arms doesn't mean I'm all gross and want toe jam in my Cheetos). By the time I finished drying them, my stomach cramping had eased, but I didn't feel hungry anymore. I went outside, found a secluded spot under a tree, sat in the grass, and read my science book.

I'M SURE A LOT OF PEOPLE THINK

it would be cool to live inside a theme park. And if that theme park was Disney World, I'm sure they would be right. Though I've never been there, I imagine living in Stagecoach Pass is probably not a whole lot like living in Disney World. It's more like living in Disney Shanty Town.

We'd moved into the small apartment over the Stagecoach Pass Saloon and Steakhouse because running a theme park is apparently a twenty-four-hour-a-day job; you never know when an ancient toilet might explode—hopefully not with someone on it—or a kid might get bitten by a crazed bunny. Because the apartment is located right on top of the steakhouse, I can hear the noisy player piano in the bar every night as I fall asleep.

The only main-course options on the menu at the steakhouse are steak and a burger, both served with cowboy beans, cornbread, and coleslaw. For the adventurous, there is fried rattlesnake or Rocky Mountain oysters for appetizers. I tried the fried rattlesnake on my first day here, and I wasn't all that impressed—it pretty much just tasted like little fried pieces of fried stuff. I didn't much care to try the Rocky Mountain oysters, though. I've had this longstanding rule of not eating private parts, and it's served me well so far.

The Saloon and Steakhouse is the first wooden building you see when you enter Stagecoach Pass after parking in the giant dirt lot, which is only a quarter full on the busiest days. Next to the steakhouse is a shooting gallery, where the fake guns have such poor aim that no one can hit the little bull's-eyes attached to plastic cactuses, wild-eyed cowboy cutouts, and stuffed, patchy-haired bobcats. Across from the shooting gallery is the tiny museum and the main souvenir shop, which sells things like drink coasters and shot glasses with cactuses on them, lollipops with scorpions inside them (yeah, like anyone would eat *that*), and postcards of the Grand Canyon—I guess so people can pretend they visited the Grand Canyon instead of Stagecoach Pass. Not that I blame them.

The main dirt road—surprisingly called Main Street—that runs through Stagecoach Pass winds a corner after the shooting gallery, and there stands a theater that shows old black-and-white westerns all day long. Maybe like one person is always sitting in there, probably just to soak up the air conditioning.

Next to the movie theater is the soda shop that sells old-fashioned candy and ice cream. It's run by a white-haired guy named Henry who's worked there since Stagecoach Pass opened and who never gets anyone's order right—ask for a single strawberry cone and he gives you a triple chocolate. He's like a hundred years old and completely senile, but he always remembers my name for some reason. I guess I'm pretty memorable—must be the red hair.

If you walk farther down the dirt road, you'll find a jail. People can pay ten dollars to have someone arrested for reasons like eating their boogers and having bad breath. I already had Dad arrested for chronic farting, and I didn't have to pay for it either because my parents run the place (VIP here). I'm planning on having Mom arrested for being a yellow sissy britches.

Across from the soda shop is a petting zoo with three goats, two sheep, four rabbits, two chickens, and Spaghetti, an extremely old mutant llama with a giant tumor growing out of his head. The lady who runs the petting zoo, Denise, told my parents the tumor can't be removed because he's too old and any surgery could kill him. Poor Spaghetti—the kids are scared of him and prefer to pet the other animals. But Spaghetti and I have a special connection.

Toward the back of Stagecoach Pass is the gold mine, run by a cranky old man named Bob who clearly hates children. When they ask him if the gold is real, he's supposed to tell them "It's real Stagecoach Pass gold!" with a cheesy southern accent. Instead he usually says in a mean-sounding Philadelphia accent, "It's real gold spray-painted rocks, genius," or "If it was real, do you think I'd be here letting you dig it up?" or simply "Shut your pie hole."

You can have your palm read by Madame Myrtle, the park's psychic. She had a hard time figuring out my future, though. I asked her to read the bottom of my foot, but all she told me was that I had a lot of callouses and she liked my blue sparkly nail polish.

Kids have the choice to ride either a thousand-year-old donkey named Billy or a washed-up circus camel named Fred on the dirt trail that winds through the ten-acre piece of desert that sits behind Stagecoach Pass.

The rest of Main Street is littered with empty buildings and storefronts that used to house things like a photography studio for taking old-fashioned portraits and a mechanical bull ride you could pay five dollars to try. The mechanical bull still sits in the room, broken down and looking forlorn. I once walked through Stagecoach Pass and counted all the empty buildings. There are seventeen—more than the buildings in operation.

When Stagecoach Pass opened sixty years ago, it was probably quite the tourist attraction, sitting way out in the middle of the desert. The city has caught up to it, though, and besides the patch of desert that sits behind it, and the tiny border of desert that runs around it, it is completely surrounded by buildings and houses—a strange little time capsule in the middle of a big city.

That first day after school, I walked into the soda shop, stomping my dusty purple flats all the way in to try to bring them back to their bright color.

"Is there a marching band in here?" Henry called.

"No." I frowned. "My shoes are all dirty."

"That's the desert for you," Henry said. "What can I get you, little Aven?"

"Just a single scoop of mint chip in a bowl, please."

While I waited, I looked at the framed pictures of tarantulas lining one wall of the soda shop.

"Someone must have really liked tarantulas to put all these pictures up," I said to Henry as he scooped my ice cream.

He laughed. "Of course! You do, Aven."

"I don't know anything about tarantulas."

Henry chuckled and waved a hand at me, like I was acting silly.

"No really, I've never seen a tarantula before in my life," I said.

He just smiled and shook his head. "You can't fool me, Aven." He handed me my ice cream—a double scoop of vanilla. Oh, well.

I carefully picked the paper bowl up between my chin and shoulder. I walked out of the soda shop and sat in a rocking chair on the front porch to eat my vanilla—which I don't even like—ice cream.

I dreaded going home and being subjected to more of the interrogation about my day Mom had started in the car. There simply wasn't anything to tell.

After a few bites, I threw my ice cream in the trash. I had already explored most of the park, so I decided to make my way around the back of the soda shop and see what was behind the buildings.

I found a narrow dirt (of course) trail that wound through the small strip of desert that surrounded Stagecoach Pass. I followed it until I came to a small building—more like a shack. It was at the very edge of the property, which was bordered with a chain-link fence. Behind the fence I could see the back of the large grocery store Mom and I had already visited.

I walked around the shack, noting the seven **DO NOT ENTER** signs nailed to the outside. The old wooden doors had been padlocked, probably a very long time ago, because the metal handle on one had completely rotted off the wood, and the lock was still hanging with it on the other handle.

I tried pushing on the handle with my side, but the door was so stiff, I could barely move it. I needed someone's hands to pull it open. I peeked in one of the windows. Through the film of dirt, I could vaguely make out stacks of boxes and what looked like old props. Why on earth would someone padlock the doors and put seven **DO NOT ENTER** signs on this building filled with nothing but junk?

I had to get in there.

"WHY IS YOUR WHOLE LUNCH IN here?" Mom asked as she rummaged through my school bag. She narrowed her eyes at me, gripping the bag like it was evidence in a murder trial. "Didn't you eat anything?"

"Yeah, I had an ice cream over in the soda shop." I opened the fridge with my chin and shoulder, pulling on the special strap Dad had installed, opened the produce drawer with my foot, and lifted out a small bag of carrots.

I could feel Mom's frown on my back. "You're going to have to eat in front of the other kids at some point, Aven."

"I know. I just wasn't hungry today."

"Are you embarrassed, honey?" she asked. I could hear the sadness in her voice.

"It was my first day, Mom. I just felt nervous, so I didn't have any appetite."

"Well, I hope that's all it was," she said. "Because you have nothing to feel embarrassed about."

"I know that." I shut the fridge and turned around. "You want to hear something weird?"

"Always."

"Henry in the soda shop kept telling me I love tarantulas."

"Well, do you?" she asked.

I laughed. "I don't know. Why would he tell me that?"

"He has dementia, sweetheart. He doesn't think clearly anymore. Who knows what might have been going on in his mind when he said that?"

"He just really seemed to think I was someone who would like tarantulas, I guess. He also gave me vanilla today. Yuck."

Mom sighed. "I know. Dad and I don't have the heart to replace him, though. He's worked here for sixty years. How could we do that?"

"No, that would be awful," I agreed. "I can learn to like vanilla."

Mom smiled at me. "Oh, I almost forgot," she said. "I have a surprise for you."

I followed her down the short hallway to my room, carrying my bag of baby carrots between my chin and shoulder. The apartment had only two little bedrooms, one bathroom, a living area, and a kitchen—a lot smaller than our house in Kansas.

"Ta-da," she announced as we entered my tiny room.

"Wow," I said, sitting down in front of the new computer she had set up at my desk.

"Dad and I thought you could use a new one. And we found a keyboard with extra large keys for pre-schoolers. Might be easier to use than our keyboard."

I slipped my feet out of my flats and tapped my toes on the keys. "Yeah, I think this will work great. Thanks, Mom."

I hit the power button with my toes and waited for it to start up.

"One more thing," Mom said. She told me an address to type. "Your own blog!" she cried.

I stared at the page. "Cool."

"Dad set it up for you. We know you love to read Emily and Brittney's blogs, so we thought you should have one, too. It might be a good way for them to keep up on everything that's going on with you here."

"What should I blog about?"

"What do Emily and Brittney blog about?"

"Brittney mostly blogs about fantasy books, and Emily is trying to be a restaurant critic."

Mom smiled. "Why don't you blog about soccer? That reminds me—did you find out when tryouts are?"

"Not until spring, unfortunately. I kind of hoped they would have soccer in the fall."

"That stinks," Mom said. "Well, you and Dad will just have to keep practicing together until then." Dad had already set up the new goal in the rodeo arena, and we had gone out there together early one morning before the sun could cook us. Despite the ball getting all dusty while we played, it had been kind of fun.

"Yeah," I said. "Yeah, we will." Dad had enrolled me in soccer when I was in second grade. Prior to that, our attempts at several "dad" activities had mostly ended in failure, or worse, disaster. The time he tried to teach me how to fish immediately comes to mind— think fishing hooks in toes and ears and everywhere else except a fish's mouth. Then there's the time he took me camping. The whole trip stunk—no showers, no soft mattress, smelly campfire, no TV. I know you were thinking I was going to say it stunk for some reason that had to do with me not having arms. Nope. It stunk because I hate camping.

When Dad decided he just *had* to teach me a sport or he would die from never having any sort of bonding activity with me beyond watching old episodes of *The Lone Ranger* and eating chili together, soccer was the obvious choice. I have had nightmares about trying out for other sports at school—usually they involve people throwing various balls at me (footballs, baseballs, basketballs, take your pick) and those balls hitting me in the head or face while everyone in school watches. Not pretty. Soccer, though—that's a sport I can manage.

Mom let out a big sigh. "Now I've got to get over to that stupid gold mine and talk to Bob." She said his name with a sneer. "You know he actually smacked a gold pan out of a four-year-old's hand today because he kept picking the quartz out instead of the gold. Dad had to give the whole family free ice cream and T-shirts." She threw her hands up in exasperation.

"He's pretty awful," I said. "Any day now I expect he'll hit a toddler over the head with one of those pans, and then you'll have to give the family a whole lot more than ice cream and T-shirts."

Her eyes grew huge with alarm like I was Madame Myrtle and had just foretold the actual future. I giggled as she stormed out of my room, having sufficiently worked herself up to lay into Bob, mumbling something about how he better get his butt in line or she'd be putting her foot in it. I was happy Mom was working with Dad at the park. She seemed to enjoy it, and it would give her something to do while I was at school during the day.

I turned and stared at the screen. I typed my first blog post.

> School sucks and it's hotter outside than the dishwasher's steam cycle. But much less steamy. And it doesn't smell like soap. At least my arms aren't hot, though. Ha-ha. Yeah, that's because I don't have any.

I posted it and nodded at the screen with satisfaction. Then I sat on my bed and munched on the carrots while I worked on my homework. My teachers had all been nice enough, but I didn't want them giving me special treatment. I could tell they all wanted to. The worst had been when Mr. Jeffries, my art teacher, had asked the class if someone would pair up with me to help me get my paints ready. I couldn't have felt more put on the spot than if he had asked me to tap dance while balancing the paints on my head. I told him I didn't need help and could get my paints ready myself.

The whole class had watched me the entire time, trying to pretend they weren't watching, as I had collected my supplies and arranged them at my workspace. It took me at least twice as long as most people to do things like this, and yet I still managed to be the very first person in the room to have all my paints ready. I guess the other kids had been too busy observing. I tried not to let it get to me. I reminded myself throughout the day that curiosity was normal; I shouldn't let it bother me.

I missed my friends back home. No one ever treated me like I was different in Kansas. Of course I'd had to deal with the usual stares when I'd go out places, but never at school. I especially missed Emily. I wished we were sitting on my bed together, working on our homework, listening to some terrible pop song Emily loved, giggling about something stupid. But it was just me.

I sighed as I wrote out a math problem, nimbly holding the pencil between my toes. I loved math. After all, it was just problem-solving. From the time I was little, my parents had trained me to be an extreme problem-solver—like a problem-solving ninja. Even when it took me an hour to get a bathing suit on once when I was eight, they still hadn't done it for me. And I never had trouble getting my bathing suit on again. They were determined I would grow up to be a totally self-sufficient, problem-solving expert. I only wished I could solve the problem of how to make friends in a sea of kids who thought I was a freak.

THE NEXT DAY AT LUNCHTIME, I headed to the bathroom again to wash my feet. But this time, when I finished, I couldn't bring myself to leave. I thought about the other kids watching me while I ate, and my stomach cramped up painfully like it had the day before.

I locked myself in the handicapped stall and sat down. I pulled out my lunch and began eating, careful not to put my bare foot on the floor or drop my peanut butter and jelly sandwich, which would pretty much put an end to eating that day.

I always ate peanut butter and jelly at school. That's because peanut butter and jelly sticks together nicely. A turkey sandwich with lettuce, tomato, and cheese would be a disaster for me. I'd seen people who couldn't even eat turkey sandwiches with their hands without stuff falling out all over the place. I imagined trying to eat a sandwich like that in the bathroom, everything ending up on the gross floor except a single slice of mayonnaise-y bread I still managed to hold in my toes. I giggled at the thought.

As I munched on a carrot, I heard a couple of girls enter the bathroom. They were talking about some cute boy who had looked at one of them. I rolled my eyes and continued crunching on my carrot, hopeful it wasn't as loud to them as it was to me. A ton of boys had looked at me. Heck, boys were looking at me all the time, but I didn't think this was how the boy had looked at this girl.

When the bathroom was finally quiet and the girls had obviously left, I packed up my stuff and headed to class.

Art went a little better that day. Mr. Jeffries had apparently learned his lesson and didn't make any more pleas for help on my behalf.

The day after that, I couldn't bring myself to eat in the bathroom stall again. Besides the fact that it was flat-out gross, it was also depressing. Instead, I told myself to stop being such a coward, and I ignored my cramping stomach. I sat in the same secluded spot I had sat reading on my first day, and I ate my lunch, hoping no one would notice me. Some kids did pass by and sneak glances at me, but I tried not to pay any attention to them or to my thumping heart. At one point, a group of three girls walked up to me as I took a bite of my string cheese, carefully held between two toes. I dropped it on my napkin, not wanting them to see me eat it like that. I smiled nervously at the girls.

"Um, hi," one of the girls said. She had on a cute flowery tank top with spaghetti straps, and once again I felt the sting of being too afraid to wear such a thing.

"Hi," I said. "How are you?" I hoped desperately I didn't have any food on my face because I wasn't about to wipe my mouth with my foot or shoulder.

"We're good," another girl said. She was also very stylish, dressed in a cute green tank top and jean shorts. "How are you?"

"Good," I said, hoping the girls weren't just here out of curiosity. I scolded myself for assuming that was all that interested them. Maybe they were going to ask me to come sit with them so I didn't have to eat lunch alone.

"Is it okay . . . um, is it okay if we ask you what happened to your arms?" flowery-tank-top girl asked.

Yep, curiosity. I sighed. I didn't have the energy to tell them my arms were chopped off in a guillotine or something like that. And these girls seemed far too nervous. I would probably terrify them. Instead, I recited, "I have an extremely rare genetic disorder that causes malformation of the limbs."

The girls looked alarmed. "Is it contagious?" green-tank-top girl asked.

I gazed at the girl, searching her face to see if she was serious. I imagined passing my armlessness on to other people, their fully grown arms shrinking and shriveling and getting sucked up into their shoulders with a terrible slurping sound after I touched them. I slowly shook my head and spoke carefully so she would understand. "No, it's genetic. That means you have to be born with it."

The girls' faces all relaxed as flowery-tank-top girl said, "Oh, that's good. It was nice meeting you." I watched them walk away.

I looked down at my string cheese. The girls hadn't met me at all. They hadn't even asked me my name. No, what they had met were my missing arms. It was all they had seen and all that had interested them. And not just out of curiosity but because they were afraid—afraid they could catch it from me.

I didn't feel hungry anymore. I packed up the rest of my lunch, stuck it in my bag, and waited for the bell to ring.

BEHIND STAGECOACH PASS, AT THE
center of the dirt trail where Billy and Fred lug around
an endless stream of screaming children, stands a
mountain. It's a tiny mountain. Well, maybe mountain
is too generous a word for it. It's more of a hill—a
mighty hill that desperately wants to be a mountain,
but a hill nonetheless.

I like to walk down Main Street in the early evening as the air starts to cool and the sky turns colors
I've never seen before. I stop for a quick visit with Spaghetti, the poor mutant llama—Spaghetti, who understands how it feels to be ostracized by the other kids.

If no one is in the soda shop, Henry might be
sitting outside on the front porch in one of the old

rocking chairs. He always waves at me and says, "Good evening, little Aven."

I pretend to be captivated by something way off in the distance as I pass by Bob at the gold mine, careful not to make eye contact with him.

Though a trail winds around the hill, no trail goes up the hill, so I navigate around cactuses that look like ping-pong paddles and giant troll-doll hair to get to the top, watching the ground for scorpions and rattlesnakes. The soles of my shoes pick up lots of little cactus needles as I walk, and mom has to dig them out with tweezers when I get home.

At the top of the hill stands an enormous saguaro cactus. It's probably as tall as about ten of me standing one on top of the other. It has seven impressive arms reaching up to the colorful evening sky.

Show-off.

Dad says the saguaro is likely over two hundred years old (he had to Google saguaros to find that out). I like to sit on the hard desert dirt and think of all the things that have happened in this saguaro's life—it stood here when Stagecoach Pass was built sixty years ago and when Arizona became a state over a hundred years ago. It stood here as the Civil War raged on the other side of the country, when women were finally granted the right to vote, and when Martin Luther King Jr. gave his "I have a dream" speech. Billions of people have been born and have died in its lifetime. And, of course, it stood here on the day I was born and will likely be standing on the day I die.

I am an entirely insignificant event in the life of this cactus. I try to remember that as the sky darkens and the lights of Scottsdale and Phoenix brighten the earth—millions of lights for millions of people. And then there's just me, sitting in the dirt on a mighty hill being circled by a poor old donkey and a tired camel.

So, after all, did it really matter that the kids at school didn't talk to me? That they probably wished I wasn't there making them feel uncomfortable? That they were afraid of me?

It shouldn't have. I didn't want it to. But it did.

I DECIDED TO SPEND MY NEXT LUNCH

period in the library. I knew I could get there two different ways: the busy route, which went right past the cafeteria, and the quiet route, which went the long way around the office. I opted for the longer, quieter route—anything to avoid more stares.

As I rounded the corner, I nearly tripped over a boy sitting on the sidewalk up against the wall. I glanced down. He was eating his lunch all by himself. I looked away and mumbled, "Sorry," as I hurried toward the library.

As I walked away, I heard him say softly behind me, "That's okay."

I entered the library and set my bag down on a table. I glanced around—I only saw one other student and a couple of librarians. Most kids probably liked to use their lunch period to, I don't know, eat lunch and socialize and all that.

I felt a pang of loneliness as I scanned a row of books, searching for an exciting adventure story to take me away. I pulled out a couple books with my foot and carried them between my chin and shoulder to the table. I carefully set them down as quietly as I could.

I sat down and opened *Journey to the Center of the Earth*. Back home in Kansas, my great-grandma had gotten me an e-reader for Christmas. That e-reader was like a revelation for me. No more cumbersome pages; I could just slide my toe effortlessly across the screen to turn the page. But I still liked to pick up paper books from time to time because I didn't want to get out of page-turning practice. After all, I couldn't get all my schoolbooks on my e-reader.

Before I had finished the first page of my book, I heard a dog barking. I looked around, wondering why a dog would be in the library. I didn't see one anywhere, but I did see a boy watching me from the far side of the room. He looked away when our eyes met. I felt my cheeks grow hot as I turned my attention back to my book. He was probably staring out of curiosity like everyone else.

I heard another bark. It seemed to be coming from the direction of the boy. I glanced that way. I still didn't see any dog, but then the oddest thing happened: the boy barked at me. I didn't know whether to make eye contact with him or look away. I didn't know if something was wrong with him, like he was insane and could attack me at any moment, or if he was making fun of me in some completely bizarre way.

I decided to go back to my book. I excelled at ignoring people. I read for a couple of minutes before he barked again. Maybe I wasn't so good at ignoring people after all. I got up from my seat and walked toward him. He stared down at his book as I came closer. When I was finally standing in front of him, he slowly raised his eyes to my face, his lightly freckled cheeks blazing red, much like mine. "I'm sorry," I said slowly, "but are you . . . *barking* at me?"

I hadn't thought the guy's cheeks could get any redder, but they did. "Yeah," he stammered. "I'm sorry."

"Are you making fun of me?"

"Oh, no." He barked again. "I can't help it. I have Tourette syndrome."

I stared at him. "You have what?"

"Tourette syndrome," he repeated.

"What's that?"

The boy cleared his throat, barked and then said, "Tourette syndrome is a neurological disorder that causes involuntary motor or oral tics." He tugged on his messy, light brown hair in a nervous way.

I couldn't believe it—he had just recited his well-rehearsed explanation of his disability like I had done a hundred times before.

The boy looked from my face down to my non-arm area and exclaimed, "Whoa! You don't have any arms," in a *Were you aware of this fact?* sort of way.

His response to my missing arms was so direct, I had to smile. I glanced down and shrieked, causing him to jump a little. "Oh my gosh! I knew I was forgetting something today."

He sat there expressionless for a little while like he didn't know what to make of my bad joke. "How did you lose your arms?" he finally asked.

I shrugged. "I'm always misplacing stuff. Probably left them in the fridge when I got the milk out this morning. Really, they could be anywhere."

He grinned, then barked. "Were they amputated for some reason?" Usually people pretended they didn't notice my missing arms at all or acted all weird about it like those girls at lunch yesterday. It was a relief to have someone be so honest about the thoughts in his head.

I sat down at the table and leaned in close to him. He did not lean away from me. Instead, he leaned closer. "Have you ever been to the circus?" I asked before beginning my newest story—one I hadn't gotten to try out yet.

"No."

"Well," I said, "I used to be a trapeze artist. You know what that is, right?"

"Don't they, like, hang from ropes and stuff? Like acrobats or something?"

"Oh, they do a lot more than that. They do all kinds of tricks—like swinging from the ropes and doing flips in the air before grabbing another rope. They often work in pairs with one person holding the other person and swinging them up in the air or catching them after they've done a flip. Supercool stuff like that."

"Awesome." He was clearly impressed. "How did you do that with no arms, though? Did you, like, use your legs? Like a monkey?"

"No, I used the arms I *used* to have."

His light hazel eyes grew wide. "*Used* to have?"

I nodded. "Yeah. You see, my partner and I were trying out this new routine. I was going to flip three times in the air before he caught me by the arms. But the speed I needed to do such an amazing stunt was just too much. When he caught me . . ." I closed my eyes and breathed in deeply for drama. "When he caught me, my shoulder sockets came loose and my arms tore right off."

He gaped at me. "What?"

"It was awful," I went on. "Him just hanging up there holding some arms, blood showering the screaming audience. It was all over the news. Didn't you see it?"

We continued staring at each other, like we were in a contest to see who would blink first. Finally he grinned a little. Then a lot. Then he started laughing. "You're totally joking," he said and laughed even louder. I was happy he found my story funny.

"Keep it down, Connor," a librarian said as she walked by with a stack of books. "This is still a library."

He smiled at the librarian, then barked at her. As she walked away, he turned back to me, still chuckling. "That's Ms. Wright. She's super nice. She lets me sit in here during lunch even though my tics are sometimes really loud. Hardly anyone's in here during lunch, so it's the best part of my day." He tugged at his hair again. "So is that what you tell everyone? That your arms were torn off in a circus accident?"

"No, that's my newest story. I was born like this.

The truth is totally boring so I make up stories for fun. I have lots of them if you'd like to hear."

He nodded. "What's your name?"

"Aven."

"I'm Connor. I would shake your hand, but . . . " He motioned toward my armless area, blinking his eyes rapidly and barking as he did so.

"But you have horrible warts all over your hands," I said.

Connor laughed again. "You're funny, Aven."

I blushed. My skin is so fair even the slightest flush to my cheeks makes me bright red—I was probably neon right now. I once Googled "excessive blushing" and found out there's a terrifying name for my condition: idiopathic craniofacial erythema. I went to school the next day and dramatically announced, "I have idiopathic craniofacial erythema!" My teacher called my mom out of concern for my health that evening.

Connor blinked rapidly and barked again. "How long have you been going here?"

"Just started a few days ago," I said. "My family and I moved from Kansas."

"Kansas," Connor repeated. "Ever see any tornadoes?"

"Sure. We had a storm cellar and everything. A lot of people do."

"Did you ever have to get in it?"

"Oh, yeah," I said. "But luckily our house never got destroyed or anything."

"I thought you were going to tell me some crazy story about your house getting swirled up in a tornado with you in it or something," he said.

"No, I just tell stories like that about my arms. Though, come to think of it, losing my arms in a tornado would be a great story. I can see how a tornado could suck them right up." I pondered this for a moment. "I'll have to think of one later."

"Cool. I can't wait to hear it," he said. "I'd love to see a tornado." Connor jerked his head and barked again. "So why'd you move here anyway?"

"My parents run a place called Stagecoach Pass. We actually live there, if you can believe that."

"That's so cool," Connor said.

"Not really."

"No, it is. I live in an apartment really close to it. My parents took me once, but I haven't been in a long time."

"Well, you're not missing anything," I said. "So don't worry."

"Do they still do gunfights?"

"Yes."

"And camel rides?"

"Yes."

"And gold—"

"Yes."

"Cool," Connor said.

"You should stop over sometime," I told him. "Since you haven't been there in a while and you live so close. I can even get you a free ice cream cone."

He looked uncomfortable at the invitation. "Maybe. I don't really like to go out a lot."

"Oh, okay." I watched him as he continued to blink his eyes rapidly. "So all these things you do," I said. "Like the barks and the eyes and the jerks and all that, that's from your . . . "

"Tourette's. Yeah, it really sucks."

"You can't just, like, hold it in? Like a yawn?"

Connor nodded. "I can for a little while. I've tried before—to act normal just at school and hold in all my tics. It hurts, though. It's really, really hard to hold them in like that, and then when I'd get home it would be a tic explosion like you can't imagine. It really upset my mom, and I would be so exhausted from holding them in all day and then letting them out all night that I couldn't even do my homework or anything. So I don't try to hold them in anymore."

"Can you take medicine for it or anything like that?"

Connor shook his head. "I tried some medication and it didn't help. It made it worse, actually. And it made me supertired all the time. I could barely get out of bed."

"Isn't there anything else you can do?"

"Sort of," Connor said. "Before my parents got divorced last year, I was seeing a therapist. But my mom's too busy working now, so I don't go anymore."

I frowned. "How do the other kids treat you?"

"Okay. I guess most everyone is used to it by now. Sometimes I get made fun of—I'll hear kids barking in the hall or wherever. And some days, when the tics are extra bad, I hear some of them laughing. One time I heard a couple of kids giggling behind me in class, and when I turned around they were mimicking me—jerking their heads."

I cringed. "That's terrible."

Connor shrugged. "I think some of them assume I do it for attention, but I don't care. Most people I meet think I'm doing it deliberately at first."

I bit the inside of my cheek. I had thought that, too. "Do you have any friends?" I asked.

Connor shrugged again. "I've only been here a year. My mom and I moved to the apartment near

Stagecoach Pass after we sold our house, so I had to change schools. It's been kind of rough coming to a new school and all that. I guess that's why I spend a lot of time in the library. What about you?"

"I haven't made any friends here, but I had a lot of friends back home in Kansas. I guess because we all grew up together, no one thought I was weird or anything. They were just used to it."

Connor nodded. "Yeah. I had a couple of friends in my old school who didn't get annoyed by my tics, but I don't really see them anymore now that we live so far apart." Connor rolled his eyes and blinked rapidly. "Has anyone been mean to you?"

"No, not really. They just act weird around me, you know, like they don't know whether to look or not, to ask about it or not. But no one has talked to me like I'm an actual person."

Connor nodded in understanding. "People act like that around me, too. Except I think it's that they don't know whether to laugh or not. Like they're not sure if they're being mean or whatever. Some people just ignore it, like it's not even happening. I guess I like that the best."

"Some people do that to me, too, but in my case it's kind of ridiculous," I said. Connor jerked his head and laughed. "Yeah, like my armlessness is something that could slip by someone. I mean, how unobservant do you have to be to not notice that someone doesn't have arms?"

"I'm pretty unobservant and it only took me about a minute."

"My point exactly." The bell rang for class to start, and my happy mood sank. I wanted to stay here with Connor. It was nice to have someone to talk to besides my parents. "I guess I better go get my bag." I stood up from the table and looked down at him. "I'm glad I stopped in here today."

Connor looked back up at me and smiled. "Me, too."

ON SUNDAY AFTERNOON, I WROTE
another blog post.

When you have a malformation (yuck, I hate that word) like I do, you definitely have to deal with the usual looks. The most popular look I get is the one I like to call the "I'm so cool nothing fazes me, not even your missing arms" look. These are the people who pretend they don't notice my missing arms. You could also call this the "Sure, I'm totally used to seeing people with no arms" look or the "I have tons of armless friends" look. These people are just way too blasé about it. I mean, come on, you really don't notice my missing arms? Because I can tell you do by how you refuse to look at my torso like the whole sun is sitting on my chest. Just go ahead and look, for goodness sake. Look and ask questions if you want. These people try way too hard.

Then there's the look I like to call "Oh my gosh, I'm staring at your armless area. Just kidding, no, I'm not. Now I'm staring. No, I'm not." These are the people I can clearly see staring at me out of the corner of my eye, but as soon as I look at them, they look away. Seriously people, you're not fooling anyone. Just keep on staring—it's okay to be curious. Everyone is.

There's also the dreaded pity look—the "Oh, you poor thing with no arms" look. These people not only look at me, but they give me a pitifully sad smile when I make eye contact with them. They should save those looks for starving, homeless orphans. Being armless isn't that bad.

And then there is the worst look of all. I have to deal with it because it almost always comes from little kids who haven't learned manners yet. It's the

"I can't stop staring at you because you're a freak"
look. Sometimes these looks end in screams and
kids running away.

I stopped typing. The post sounded all light-hearted and ha-ha funny. But I didn't write that I ignore these looks to the best of my ability. I didn't write that I pretend they don't bother me, but even after thirteen years of seeing them, they still hurt. I also didn't write that the last time I got one of these looks was just the day before, while I was grocery shopping with Mom.

Mom likes to take me grocery shopping with her. She says it's because I need to learn how to grocery shop on my own, but I really think it's because she likes having a child slave to command. So Mom basically makes me handle all the groceries in the store—I have to get the canned tomatoes from the bottom shelf, the soy sauce from the top shelf (I'm so flexible, it would blow your mind), the cereal from the middle shelves, the bag of apples from the produce department (we go with bagged produce so I'm not putting my feet all over the fresh food in front of people), and yes, even the rotisserie chicken. The rotisserie chicken was sort of a disaster, but that's not the point of this story. The fact that it takes us three hours to grocery shop isn't the point either. Sometimes I wish Mom had some other hobby besides teaching Aven how to do stuff.

So I was in the cereal aisle trying to slide this box of Corn Puffs out from the shelf with my foot. I had just finally gotten it wedged between my head and shoulder, but as I stood up and turned to drop it into the cart, I caught this little girl standing in the aisle giving me the dreaded "I can't stop staring at you because you're a freak" look.

I stared back at her for a moment. "You got a problem with Corn Puffs?" I said.

Her mom's head shot up from reading the label on a box of instant oatmeal. She saw what was going on and grabbed her cart and daughter and scurried away.

I acted all cool, like I couldn't have cared less about it. But I still remember it happening. I remember every time it happens.

When I was done writing my post, Dad asked me to help him put some fresh paint on the flat wooden pictures standing by the front entrance of the park—the kind with cutouts people can stick their heads through for photographs. I seriously doubted anyone took pictures with the faded, wooden figures, but I agreed to go with him because I'm such a good daughter.

I could see why he wanted to freshen them up; the paint was so faded you could hardly tell what they were anymore, and one of them looked like you were sticking your head through a giant boob—not exactly the family-friendly image we were going for.

Dad put a chair out for me to sit on while I painted with my foot. My painting skills aren't exactly the finest, but I can manage large simple pictures. Just don't expect me to paint your portrait unless a stick-figure face is acceptable.

As I worked on turning the boob back into a small hill with a barrel cactus on top of it, I saw Connor walking over the bridge that connected the parking lot to the park—the bridge was built to go over a wash. Washes are like empty riverbeds that run all over North Scottsdale so that when it rains, the water can flood the city in an orderly manner.

Connor didn't have to go through a kiosk or anything like that as he entered the park because admission was free—all the money made was from paying for the many "attractions" we had. *Pfft*. If you could call them that.

"Hey, Connor," I said as he walked up to me, barking a few times on his way. "You came."

"Hi, Aven," he said, looking around, squeezing his hands together. "There aren't very many people here."

"Oh, this place is always dead," I told him.

Connor seemed relieved.

Dad looked up from painting the gun in a cowboy's hand. I had thought it was a sea cucumber, but a gun made a lot more sense—why would the cowboy be pointing a sea cucumber at people as they entered the park? And where would a cowboy in the middle of the desert get a sea cucumber from anyway? "Who's this, Aven?" Dad asked.

"Dad, this is Connor. We met at school."

Dad reached out his hand and Connor shook it. "Nice to meet you, Connor."

"Do you mind if I take a break?" I asked Dad.

He looked at my handiwork so far. "It definitely looks less boobish, so I guess you're free to go." I handed him my paintbrush, slipped my shoe back on, and walked off with Connor down Main Street.

Connor suddenly chuckled beside me. "It's just so cool that you live here."

I scowled at the comment. "So what have you been up to?"

"Oh, nothing," he said. "My mom's working all

weekend, and I got tired of playing video games so I thought I'd walk over and see if you were here."

It made me feel good that he had come here just to see me, especially since he had mentioned not liking to go out a lot. "I like to play video games."

He looked surprised. "Really?"

"Yes," I said, annoyed at his look of surprise. "I can play. I bet I could kick your butt at just about any game."

"Are you challenging me? Because pretty much all I do when I'm at home is play video games. I'm like a professional video-game player."

"We'll just see about that," I said. "Does your mom always work on the weekends?"

He shrugged. "Yeah, she works all the time. She has two jobs." He shrugged again, and I realized the shrugging was another one of his tics. I wondered how many different tics he had.

"What does your mom do?" I asked.

"She's an ER nurse."

"That's cool."

"I guess," Connor said. "Except I never get to see her."

"I'm sorry." I didn't know what else to say, so I walked up to the porch of the soda shop and sat down in one of the rocking chairs. Connor sat beside me. I tried to think of something else to talk about. "My mom took me to this cool instrument museum yesterday. Have you ever been there?"

Connor shook his head. "I don't get out much."

"Do you play any instruments?"

He shook his head again and barked. "No."

I waited for him to ask me if I did. He didn't, and I figured it was because he assumed I couldn't. "I play." I hadn't meant to say it with quite so much sass.

He looked surprised again, of course. Why were people always surprised I could do stuff? I bet I'd get surprised looks if I told people I can breathe air without help or swallow my food or pee in the toilet.

"What do you play?" he asked.

"Guitar."

"With your feet?"

"No, with my belly button."

Connor's eyes widened, then he pursed his lips in a little smirk. "You're joking again, aren't you?"

"Yes. I play with my feet, not with my belly button."

"Awesome," he said, rocking in his chair and blinking his eyes rapidly. He did look impressed. "Play for me sometime? I've got to see you play with your feet."

I shifted in my seat. "Um, sure." I didn't tell him I also wrote my own music and sang.

In fifth grade, I had come to the realization that it was far more productive for me to channel my creative storytelling into songwriting than to only use it to shock people with morbid horror stories about my armlessness. I had written several songs since then. Most of them were pretty bad—like *take an ice pick to your own ears* bad. A song I wrote about learning how to put my first bra on immediately comes to mind. A couple were possibly worth playing, but the only people I had ever played for were my parents.

"Do you ever see your dad?" I asked him.

His expression turned somber, and I was instantly sorry I had asked. "Not much."

"That's too bad." I rocked in my chair beside him.

"He and my mom used to fight about me all the time." He looked out at Main Street as he spoke. "He didn't understand why I couldn't just hold my tics in. It made him angry. He always said to me, 'Connor, why don't you just knock it off? Look at how upset you're making us. Just stop it!'

"And my therapy bills were expensive and my dad didn't want to pay for them anymore. He wanted me to just take the meds and stop ticcing, but they made me feel awful. I think my dad would have done anything to just stop my tics. And when he realized they weren't going to stop, he couldn't deal with it. So he left."

"I'm sure your parents had problems that had nothing to do with you or your tics," I said, thinking Connor's dad sounded like a real jerk.

"All their fights were always about me, my tics, my bills. I can see why they can't stand me. I can't stand myself most of the time. I wish I could hold the tics in and pretend to be normal."

I didn't know what to say to that. I was sure Connor was wrong about his parents. I couldn't imagine parents being like that. "I'm sorry. I wish I could grow arms and pretend to be normal."

The corner of his mouth tipped up a little.

"I still don't completely understand why you can't hold your tics in. I know you said it hurts, but why?"

Connor thought for a moment. "It's like when you have a bad cough. You know, when you get that tickle in your throat and you really want to cough. You can concentrate really hard on holding it in, but it's so uncomfortable and eventually you just have to cough. That's what it feels like to not tic—like this painful feeling in my chest builds and goes up to my throat until I just have to bark. Or it builds in my eyes until I just have to blink to relieve it. Then it builds again. And again. It never goes away for long. It always builds again."

"Oh," I said. "That's really weird. Why does it do that?"

Connor shrugged. "It's some kind of malfunction in my brain."

"Can you get brain surgery?"

Connor laughed. "That seems a little extreme. I guess they can do surgery, but only if the Tourette's is super-bad and dangerous. I can live with mine, so I'm not going to do any brain surgery. That would be scary."

"Yeah, I guess that would be pretty risky." I grinned at him. "I don't think I would do an arm transplant, even if it were possible. Could have some scary side effects."

Connor raised his eyebrows. "Oh, yeah? What kind of scary side effects?"

"Like, what if the arms came from a serial killer, and they just had to keep killing people, even on someone else's body? Or the arms were too dead, and then I had these zombie arms attached to my body?"

"Too dead?"

"Yeah. Or what if they had naked lady tattoos all over them? Or if they had a terrible nail fungus that slowly spread and took over my whole body?"

"You've thought about this a lot."

I sighed. "You have to think about these things in case the opportunity ever arises." I glanced over at the petting zoo and saw Spaghetti sticking his mutant head over the fence. I wondered if he was looking for me. I visited him several times a day to pet him with my foot and tell him how adorable he was—for his self-esteem. Since none of the other kids wanted to pet him, I felt like it was my sole responsibility to improve his ego.

"Come on," I said, sitting up from my rocker. "I want you to meet someone."

Connor followed me across the street. I stopped when I reached Spaghetti and nuzzled my face to his. "This is Spaghetti."

Connor patted Spaghetti's head without flinching. "He's cute."

"Spaghetti is a mutant," I said, kissing his head. "Like me."

"You shouldn't say that about yourself." Connor gave me a stern look, like he was my dad.

"I didn't mean a creepy mutant," I said. "We're, like, cool X-Men mutants."

Connor smiled. "Oh, well then that's okay."

We left Spaghetti and walked back to the soda

shop. Henry stepped out onto the porch. "I thought I saw you out here, Aven," he said.

"Hi, Henry," I said. "This is my friend, Connor." I felt a little warm fuzzy in my chest when I used the words *my friend*.

Henry smiled at Connor and then turned back to me. "You all ready for the next rodeo?"

I glanced at Connor. "I'm not going to be in any rodeo."

Henry laughed. "That'll be the day!" he said. "A rodeo without Aven! Well, say hi to Joe for me." He started to walk back inside.

"I don't know any Joe!" I called to Henry. "Do *you* know Joe?"

Henry just chuckled again and did that same little hand wave like he had when I'd told him I didn't know anything about tarantulas. "You're such a joker," he said, then turned and went back into the soda shop.

"That was weird," Connor said. "Who's Joe?"

"I don't know," I said. "The owner of the park's name is Joe Cavanaugh, but I guess no one ever sees him or seems to know anything about him. The accountant told my parents he never visits the park." I leaned in and lowered my voice. "And get this—pictures of the Cavanaughs in the museum here have been removed."

"That is strange," Connor said. "I wonder why."

"I don't know. I found this old storage shed behind the buildings, though. It has seven **DO NOT ENTER** signs on it and an old broken handle that was padlocked. I couldn't get the doors open, but you might be able to. You want to try?"

Connor nodded excitedly. "Yeah, let's go."

I led him down the short trail until we reached the old wooden shed. It looked like it was on the verge of collapse—much like several of the other buildings at the park. "See all the signs?" I said.

"Cool. I wonder what's in there."

After a few tugs and grunts, Connor was able to slide the door open enough that we could squeeze through the opening. I scraped my nose a bit on the old wooden door, and I hoped I didn't get any splinters in my face—getting them out wouldn't be fun.

Connor and I looked around at the stacks of boxes, the piles of junk, the shelves stuffed with old books and papers and props. "Where do we even begin?" I said.

I looked up and saw a box perched on top of one of the old bookshelves. The writing on it was faded and water-stained, but I could just barely make out three letters: *A, V*, a water-stained space and then an *N*. "Check out that box up there," I told Connor.

He looked up and read the letters. "*A, V, N.*" We stood a moment in silence before Connor barked, startling me. "*Aven!*" he cried.

I snorted. "Of course not *Aven.*" I thought for a moment. "*Cavanaugh!*"

"Oh, right." Connor smacked himself in the head. "Stupid." He stared at it awhile. "How do we get it down?"

I looked around the room for a ladder or something. "I could try head-butting it off the shelf," I said.

Connor laughed. "If we can find something for me to stand on, I think I can get it down."

We found a little table covered in old documents in one corner of the room. Connor moved the papers off it and dragged the table to the bookshelf. He climbed up and brought the box down, then placed it on the table and opened it. "This stuff is old," he said, pulling out a book that looked like it had been soaked in water and left to dry out in the heat repeatedly. Though it was badly damaged, we could make out the big hairy tarantula on the cover.

"More tarantula stuff," I mumbled, studying the cover.

"What's the deal with tarantula stuff?" Connor asked.

"Someone here was really into them. There are

tarantula pictures in the soda shop and a tarantula display in the museum."

Connor pulled out another book—a sketchbook. The pages made brittle crinkling sounds as Connor turned them. "Careful," I told him as a corner of one page broke off. We studied the sketches—there were several drawings of horses and Stagecoach Pass. And, of course, of tarantulas. There was also a detailed sketch of a necklace with a blue stone in it.

Connor pointed at the date on one of the pictures—1973. "Someone made these over forty years ago," he said.

We looked through the rest of the box and found some horse figurines, an old hair brush, and a glass case that reminded me of an aquarium. "Why would there be an aquarium, of all things, in here?" I said.

He shook his head. "Maybe it's for something else."

I carefully turned the fragile pages of the sketchbook with my toes, and stopped on a sketch of a tarantula. It was quite life-like—someone had spent a lot of time sketching every tiny hair on each of the eight legs. Someone who clearly had a serious interest in these giant spiders. "I think you're right."

THE NEXT DAY AFTER SCHOOL,

Mom was out checking on a beef delivery for the steakhouse and Dad was dealing with a chicken that'd gotten loose from the petting zoo when I heard a knock on the apartment door. I put down my e-reader and got up to see who was there. I had been reading a new book called *Stargirl*. I picked it for two reasons— one: It took place in the Arizona desert, and I was doing everything I could to come to terms with my new living situation. I thought reading an interesting story set here might make me view it differently. And two: It was about a girl who totally doesn't fit in with anybody. She is completely her own unique self and doesn't care what anyone thinks. I wished I could say the same thing.

I heard the bark before I even opened the door and knew it was Connor. I asked him how school went as we walked down the stairway together.

"Okay," he said. "A couple of kids barked at me. It's so embarrassing when they do that because I always bark back."

I scowled. "They wouldn't get away with that if I was around." I wasn't kidding either. This injustice would not stand. This unfairness would not be tolerated. As soon as I learned how to use nunchuks . . .

"So how was your day?" Connor asked, interrupting my little daydream. "I didn't see you at the library today."

I didn't want to tell him that I had eaten lunch in the bathroom stall. "It was okay. I didn't go to the library because my mom doesn't want me to skip lunch anymore. It makes me cranky." I gave him a serious look. "Low blood sugar."

He smiled. "It sucks we don't have any classes together. Maybe you can stop by the library after you eat lunch, even if it's only for a few minutes."

"Sure. Hey, you want to get an ice cream?" Before he could answer, I stomped up the steps of the soda shop.

I waited for him to open the door for me—not that I wasn't capable of opening it with my chin and shoulder. I just figured I'd let him be a gentleman. But he opened it begrudgingly and scowled. "I don't think I want any."

"How can you say no to free ice cream?" I said as I walked to the counter. "Didn't you know I'm a VIP here? I get free ice cream, free coleslaw, free arrests, and all the free gold spray-painted rocks my heart could ever desire."

I told Henry I wanted a double scoop of mint chip in a bowl. While he scooped the ice cream, I asked him, "Hey, what did you mean about a rodeo? When was the last time Stagecoach Pass even had a rodeo?" The arena looked like it hadn't seen a rodeo in about a hundred years.

I looked at Henry, but he was just standing there, staring at my torso. His mouth hung open. The scooper in his hand dripped ice cream onto the floor. "What?" I asked him.

"What on earth happened to your arms?" He seemed extremely concerned.

Connor and I glanced at each other. "You know I don't have any arms, Henry."

"Well, you used to!" he declared. He stared confusedly at the empty space where my arms should hang. "Did you lose those in a horse-riding accident?"

"What?"

"Yeah," he said, a little more clearly. "You were in a horse-riding accident, weren't you? That must be what happened."

"No, Henry," I said. "That's not what happened." Yeah, like a horse trampled my arms off. I mean just trampled my arms *clean* off.

Henry's face seemed to clear up a little, and he looked at Connor. "What would you like, son?"

"Nothing for him," I said. "He's on a strict diet of air."

As Henry continued scooping my ice cream, Connor whispered to me, "That was so weird."

"I know," I whispered back.

Henry placed a scoop of chocolate on the counter (darn it—I would never get that mint chip), and Connor carried it for me outside. We sat in the rocking chairs on the porch again while I ate my ice cream, holding the spoon with my toes. Connor barked at a couple of visitors passing by. They looked up at him in surprise. Then they saw me and were extra surprised.

"I hate it when people look at me," he muttered.

"Me, too."

Connor turned his attention to me. "You know, you're really good at that."

"At what?"

"That," he said. "Eating the ice cream."

"Wow. How many people do you think get complimented for how good they are at eating ice cream? I guess it's thirteen years of practice that makes me such a pro."

"It's a pretty good skill."

"Anyone could do it if they had to," I said.

Connor shrugged. "So what do you think that was all about in there?"

"I have no idea. Henry is a very confused person."

Connor and I heard a squeaking sound, and we both turned and looked at the soda shop window. Henry was cleaning it with a spray can of whipped cream. He waved at us through the smear. Connor waved back. "What's wrong with him?" he asked me.

"Mom says he has dementia. I guess it makes him confused and forgetful. He's super old, too. Obviously."

"Do you think he knows anything about the Cavanaughs?" Connor asked.

"He's worked here since forever, so if anyone knew anything about them, it would probably be him. He just doesn't seem to understand anything." I watched as Henry scowled at the glass with a *Why won't this darn window cleaner work?* sort of expression, his arms crossed. I smiled at him, and his face brightened. He disappeared, apparently not concerned about the creamy window anymore.

"Why do *you* think the Cavanaughs are so secretive?" Connor asked.

"I have no idea." I thought to myself for a moment. "Maybe they're criminals hiding from the law."

"Or maybe they're famous," Connor said.

"Yeah! Maybe they're famous members of a boy band, and they don't want anyone to know that they also dabble in western-themed amusement parks because it would ruin their cool pop-star image." Now the storytelling gears in my mind were turning. "Or maybe . . . maybe they're escaped rodeo clowns. And the rodeo clown mafia is out to get them."

Connor chuckled. "Why would they be out to get them?"

"Maybe they pulled a prank on the wrong person. You know, shot someone they shouldn't have in the face with one of those flowers that squirt water. Or hit someone on the head with a squeaky foam hammer, and that person did *not* find it funny. And now that person is out for revenge." I had to admit, the theory was totally believable.

"Or maybe someone's already gotten their revenge on the Cavanaughs," Connor said. "Maybe they're dead."

He looked so serious that little goose bumps broke out on my legs. A loud beeping sound startled me. I looked down Main Street and saw a large truck backing up to the steakhouse. Mom walked outside with a clipboard in her hands.

I turned to Connor. "Have *you* ever pulled any pranks?" I asked him, hoping to lighten the mood.

He shrugged. "My friends and I toilet-papered a teacher's house a couple of years ago." He grimaced. "We got in a lot of trouble. What about you?"

"Oh, well, no big deal, but I only pulled just the most awesome prank of all time."

"What'd you do?" Connor asked excitedly.

"Back in fourth grade, we knew we were going to have a substitute teacher one day because our teacher had to go to a funeral. So my best friend, Emily, took these arms from one of her mom's mannequins."

"Why'd she have mannequins?"

"She did a lot of sewing and stuff. I think she used them to model her clothes and take pictures or something. Anyway, Emily brought them to school in her backpack, but they were really big, so the hands stuck up out of the top."

Connor laughed. "Like zombie arms."

"Yeah, it was like *Night of the Living Dead*. So, anyway,

when we got to our classroom, our covert operation went into effect. Emily and another friend, Matthew, tried to help me secretly stuff the arms up the armholes of my long-sleeved shirt, but the tops of the arms were too big to fit up the sleeves, so we had the brilliant idea to stuff them down into the sleeves through the neck hole. The arms were so much longer than my sleeves that they stuck way out of the bottom, and I totally looked like a mutant with arms hanging down all the way to my knees.

"But we decided we'd come too far and had to go with it anyway. Matthew held both of the mannequin hands in his to hold the arms up. When the teacher called for us all to take our seats, I yelled out, 'Matthew, let go of my arms!' and he pulled on the fake arms. The idea had been that he would basically pull my arms off and then hold them up over his head in triumph, howling like some wild barbarian."

"Cool," Connor said.

"Yeah," I agreed. "It would have been. What our dumb fourth grade brains had failed to realize, though, was that because the arms wouldn't fit *up* my sleeves, they wouldn't completely fit *down* my sleeves either. The arms got stuck about halfway out. Matthew yanked on them and yanked on them, but they wouldn't come out of my sleeves."

"So what happened?"

"Since the arms weren't coming out of the sleeves and our plan was totally falling apart, I started crying out, 'Oh no, my arms! You're tearing my arms off! I can feel my arms being torn off at the sockets right now as we speak! Oh, the humanity! My poor arms!'

"Everyone was laughing, but the sub just stared at us. Matthew gave up and went to his seat, so I did, too. My sleeves were so stretched out that the arms dragged on the floor next to me as I walked and I had to maneuver around them to sit down at my desk."

Connor covered his mouth. "Oh, no. Did you get in trouble?"

"No. The sub was actually pretty nice. She didn't tattle on me to the principal or anything like that, though she did make me wear those stupid arms until lunchtime."

Connor laughed. "I bet you looked pretty silly."

"Um, yeah."

"I don't know if I'd call that the most awesome prank of all time."

"Yeah, it was kind of a fail."

"Epic fail," Connor said.

I looked down at my bowl of ice cream, already melting into a soup in the heat. I didn't feel like eating it anymore. After all, I had really wanted that mint chip. "You want the rest of this?" I asked Connor.

He shook his head.

I turned my attention back to the steakhouse. "You know, the gun show is starting in about an hour." I grinned mischievously to myself. If I had hands, they'd have been doing that evil finger-tapping thing right below my chin.

Connor gave me a confused look. "So?"

I put my ice cream down and jumped up from my rocking chair. "Follow me."

Connor followed me to the steakhouse, where Mom had finally finished up with the delivery and the truck had left. We snuck around to the back entrance and made our way to the kitchen, where cooks, busboys, and servers were all bustling around, getting ready for dinner. We stood secretly behind the giant commercial fridge.

Connor and I watched in disgust as a busboy mixed a giant vat of coleslaw with his hands, his arms buried in it all the way to his biceps. He was wearing a tank top, and we saw he had coleslaw juice dripping from his armpit hair. Connor made a sort of laughing gagging sound beside me, and I said, "Remind me to never eat the coleslaw here again."

Connor giggled and barked. "He should have little hair nets for his armpits."

"Whatchy'all doin' in here?" we heard from behind us. I whirled around to find Josephine standing behind me, her arms crossed. Josephine had already introduced herself to me on the day we moved to Stagecoach Pass. She had come to Arizona from Texas when she was only a teenager and had been working at the park since forever. She was currently serving, hostessing, and doing all kinds of jobs for the steakhouse. Seemed to me like she ran the place. She was probably eighty years old, but she could still carry one of the giant trays that held a dozen bowls of cowboy beans.

I thought quickly. "We, uh, Mom just, uh, told me to grab a couple of steaks for dinner."

Josephine gazed at me with that strange look she had given me the first time I met her. Sometimes when I was in the steakhouse, I'd catch her staring at me from across the restaurant. I was used to people staring at me, but this was different somehow.

"Well, she was just here." Josephine scratched at her cropped red hair—obviously dyed. No eighty-year-old had hair that color. "Why didn't she just take a couple then?"

I shrugged. "She forgot."

"All right. Grab them and then stay out of the way. Dinner's startin'." She plowed through the swinging doors that led to the dining room like she was on a serious mission.

Connor opened the giant commercial fridge and grabbed two thin cuts of steak. Then we rummaged through counter drawers until we found some kitchen twine and a pair of scissors. We made our way upstairs to the apartment. I was relieved to find it empty— Mom must have gone off to deal with another job or crisis. It seemed the work never ended here.

It was sloppy and haphazard, but Connor managed to dig a hole in each of the steaks, tie the twine through them and then tie them around my T-shirt sleeves, going through the arm and neck holes. I loosely draped a cardigan over my shoulders, and we made our way downstairs and out to the street to watch the gunfight, where a small crowd was already forming.

"Don't be so nervous," I told Connor as his ticcing increased.

"It's just that there are a lot of people around," he said.

Yeah, there were like four people standing by us.

We had to wait only a minute before the cowboys came out and started yelling at each other. I tapped my foot while they went through their daily spiel. Finally the moment came when the blue-shirt cowboy, who also happened to be a server at the steakhouse, raised his gun and pointed it at the cowhide-chaps cowboy, who also worked in the souvenir shop, and shouted, "When I'm done with you, there won't be anything left to snore!"

I made sure I was standing behind cowhide-chaps cowboy. Blue-shirt cowboy always missed cowhide-chaps cowboy with that first shot, but today he wouldn't miss completely. *Tee hee.*

At the moment blue-shirt cowboy fired, I cried out in pain and shrugged the cardigan dramatically off my shoulders. Connor snickered beside me with his hand over his mouth.

A couple of kids standing nearby screamed in terror, and their parents looked alarmed for about one second—all the time it took to assess the situation. Come on, it was *clearly* two steaks clumsily tied to my T-shirt and not two shot-up arms.

The cowboys stopped mid-fight and stared at me—probably not sure what to make of my steak-arms—as the little kids cried and clung to their parents' legs, afraid their arms were next. The fight was all messed up now, and people started dispersing into the rest of the park. The cowboys glared at me.

Connor draped the cardigan back over my shoulders as I smiled sheepishly at them. "Sorry," I said. "I didn't mean to mess up your show."

The next morning, the cowboys went and complained to Dad about my shenanigans. He and Mom and I sat at the little kitchen table over bowls of cereal after they busted me. "The goal, Aven," Dad said, "is to bring visitors *into* the park." He gestured dramatically toward himself. "Not scare them *out of* the park." He threw his hands back out.

I nodded in understanding. "Won't happen again."

He gave a satisfied nod and pushed his bowl away. He stood up and kissed the top of my head. "Have a good day at school, Sheebs."

After Dad left, Mom looked at me and pursed her lips. She took a bite of cereal and chewed. "It *was* a pretty good one."

"Yeah, it was," I said, and we finished breakfast together, communicating only through overly stern looks and repressed giggles.

CONNOR AND I HAD BEEN SPENDING

a lot of time together, so my parents asked me to invite him over for dinner after school.

At lunchtime, I made my way to the bathroom as usual and washed my feet. I stared at the stall. I just couldn't do it that day. I felt too happy, and I was excited to see Connor and invite him over. I didn't need another bathroom-stall lunch ruining my good mood.

So I headed to the library to find Connor, once more taking the longer, quieter route around the office. I nearly tripped over that kid again as I rounded the corner. "Gosh, I'm sorry," I said. Next time I would definitely remember to jump over him.

"That's okay," he said softly, never raising his head. I walked away, but stopped a moment to look back at him. He stared down at his sandwich and grapes lying next to him. I wondered why he would be eating out here on the hot sidewalk by himself. He looked about as forlorn and pitiful as I must have looked cowering in the bathroom stall to eat my lunch.

How could I just walk past him again, as though he were invisible? As though he were some speed bump in my way? I went back and stood over him. He looked up at me, his hoagie sandwich midway to his mouth. Sweat trickled down his brown cheeks.

"Do you mind if I sit down?" I asked.

He looked around for a second like he thought I must have been talking to the brick wall or the lamp-post nearby. When he looked back at me, he shrugged his shoulders. "Okay."

I dropped my school bag on the ground, eased the strap off from around my neck, and sat down. He watched as I carefully opened my bag with my toes and pulled out my lunch. I spread a napkin out in front of me, then lifted out my Cheetos, apple slices, granola bar, and peanut butter and jelly sandwich and arranged them on the napkin. "What's your name?" I asked as I opened the bag of Cheetos with my toes.

Instead of giving me his name, he said, "That's cool. How do you do that?"

"Lots of practice. I'm Aven."

He continued to watch with intense interest as I took out a Cheeto and popped it into my mouth. "Zion," he said.

"Like the Bible?"

"No, like *The Matrix*."

"Oh," I said, munching on my Cheeto. "What's that?"

His mouth dropped open. "Seriously? It's one of my parents' favorite movies. They love sci-fi stuff. They said I looked like Morpheus when I came out, all bald and mysterious." He frowned. "I'm not allowed to watch it, though, because it's rated *R*."

"Oh, I won't be able to either. Bummer. This Morpheus guy sounds interesting."

Zion rolled his eyes. "My parents are nuts. They also named my brother Lando, after Lando Calrissian—if you know who that is."

"Are you kidding? I am definitely allowed to watch *Star Wars*."

Zion smiled. "My parents would be impressed."

I handed (footed, actually) him a Cheeto. He took it from me without flinching. "Can I ask you something, Zion?"

"Mm-hm," he said, chewing on his Cheeto.

"Why do you eat out here on the sidewalk by yourself?"

He slowly lifted a juice box to his lips and took a long swig. "It's quiet out here."

I tilted my head and raised an eyebrow at him. "Is that the only reason?"

He stared at the ground but didn't answer me.

"It's okay," I said. "I've been eating lunch in the bathroom."

He looked up at me in surprise. "I don't want the other kids to watch me eat. Everyone likes to watch a fat guy eat. They want to see how much food he can stuff into his mouth."

"But you're not that fat," I said, then cringed at my own words. I had meant it to sound nice, but it didn't sound so nice coming out.

"It's okay. I know I am."

"Well, I think you look great," I said.

Zion handed me a grape. I took it from him with my foot and popped it into my mouth. "So why have you been eating in the bathroom?" he asked.

I swallowed my grape. "I don't want the other kids to watch me eat either."

"Why not?"

"Because they'll think I'm gross."

"No, they won't."

"Yes, they will."

"How do you know that?" Zion said.

"I just do. Once when I went to this children's museum with my parents, I sat down to play with Play-Doh at a table. Of course, I had to play with my feet, and everyone at the table stared at me."

"It *is* interesting to see."

"Then this one kid cried out, 'Gross! She's putting her feet in the Play-Doh.'"

"Kids are dumb," Zion said.

"Then his mom looked at my mom and said this: 'Would you mind not letting your daughter put her feet in the Play-Doh?'"

"Jerk," Zion muttered. "What did your mom say?"

I smiled. "She said she would make sure I used my butt cheeks instead."

Zion laughed a big, full belly laugh. "Oh, that's classic."

I ate another Cheeto. "Before that, I had never realized people thought feet were gross. Anyway, that was right before starting kindergarten. You know what the first day of kindergarten is like for a five-year-old with no arms?"

Zion grinned. "Maybe even more difficult than for a chubby five-year-old."

"Maybe. The kids asked me so many weird questions." I mimicked little kid voices. "'Did someone chop your arms off? How do you finger paint with no fingers? How do you use scissors with no hands? How will you play Duck, Duck, Goose? Are your armpits ticklish? How do you wipe peanut butter off your face?'"

Actually, what the kids really asked was, "How do you wipe poop off your butt?" but I wasn't about to tell Zion that. And no, I'm still not telling you how either, so just stop wondering.

"It was exhausting," I said.

"I bet. They asked me stuff like, 'Did you eat a skyscraper?' and 'Do you weigh more than my dad?'"

I scowled. No wonder Zion was so insecure about his weight. "I'm sorry. School really sucks sometimes, doesn't it?"

"Yeah. So can you do everything everyone else can do with your feet?"

"Mostly. I mean, things are always harder. Like the Hokey Pokey. When the song says 'Put your right hand in,' I kind of just stand there like a mannequin. And I have nightmares about flag football. Try running and grabbing someone's flag with your foot at the same time—slightly difficult."

"Yeah, I can definitely see how that would be hard."

"The only sport I can really play well is soccer."

"Are you going to try out for the soccer team in the spring?"

"I, uh, I don't know," I said. "I played soccer back home in Kansas. But, you know, I had a lot of friends and had always gone to the same school. I hardly know anyone here."

"You know me," Zion said.

I smiled and handed Zion another Cheeto. "Would you mind if I ate lunch out here with you again sometime?"

He beamed. "Okay."

Zion and I ate the rest of our lunch together that day, hidden away on the far side of the office where no one could watch us.

I FINALLY GOT TO ASK CONNOR

over as we sat on the bus together that day after school. Turns out we were on the same bus route. Mom had been driving me to and from school, but I didn't see why she needed to keep doing that when the bus would drop me off only a block from Stagecoach Pass. I knew how busy she was with stuff at the park, and I didn't want her to have to stop everything in the middle of the day to pick me up anymore.

"Is your mom working tonight?" I asked him.

"Yeah, she won't be back until early tomorrow morning."

"Then you're coming over to my house-theme-park-apartment-thingy for dinner. My parents want to meet you. I mean, I know you already met my dad briefly, but they want to meet you, like, officially, espe-cially after," I leaned in and whispered, "Steakgate."

Connor looked torn. "I can come over until dinner, but then I have to go home."

I sat back up straight. "Why? If your mom's work-ing all night, why can't you just stay?"

He shrugged and blinked his eyes rapidly. "Well, maybe I can stay. We'll see."

"I guess," I said. Connor never ate lunch, he wouldn't eat ice cream with me, and now he didn't want to have dinner at my house. I was beginning to wonder if he was starving himself. I decided to change the subject. "So I was thinking about what you said the other day—about how maybe someone, you know, offed the Cavanaughs." I whispered the word *offed* in case anyone was listening to our conversation.

Connor blinked at me. "Yeah?"

I nodded. "Yeah. And I was thinking we should maybe start considering the possibility that there is a murderer at Stagecoach Pass." Again, I whispered the word *murderer*. You can never be too careful when dis-cussing such things.

"Who?" Connor whispered.

"Could be anyone. There's this guy at the gold-mine—we call him Mean Bob because he's so mean.

Maybe he did it. Or maybe the guy who interviewed my parents—Gary the accountant. Maybe he did it."

"Why?"

"To take over the park."

"But why would he want to take over the park?"

"Money." I nodded. "It's always about money."

"How much money do you think the park makes?" Connor asked.

I actually thought the park made negative money. "Okay, maybe not money," I said. I narrowed my eyes at Connor. "Revenge."

"Revenge for what?"

"I don't know. *Yet*. But I'm going to solve this great mystery all on my own," I announced. "If you would like to assist me, you shall do so, sir."

"Okay," Connor said, not quite with the enthusiasm or the British accent I had been going for. In my mind, great detectives always had British accents.

"We should go back to the storage shed," I said.

"But there's nothing in there except papers you can barely read and old props and junk."

"Yeah, but maybe there's something hidden there. Why else would it have all those signs?"

Connor nodded. "That's true."

I tapped my feet on the bus floor. "I've never had

an exciting mystery to solve. Well, except for the time I woke up one morning with every inch of my hair, body, and bed covered in chocolate."

"Why?" Connor asked.

"A Hershey's Kiss fell out of my backpack into my bed. As I rolled around on it all night, that's what it did. Can you believe it? One Hershey's Kiss!"

Connor didn't seem that impressed with my Hershey's Kiss story. "Maybe you should ask Madame Myrtle about it," he said. "Shouldn't a psychic know about all that kind of stuff? Can't they, like, talk to dead people and stuff?"

"She just reads palms," I said. "Obviously that's not very helpful to me."

Connor smiled. "You shan't worry!" He raised a finger in the air. "We shall solve this highly mysterious mystery ourselves."

I was glad he used a terrible British accent that time.

MY PARENTS WEREN'T IN THE APARTMENT

when Connor and I got there. "You want a snack?" I asked him as we entered the tiny kitchen.

"No, thanks," he said. "I'm not really hungry."

"How can you not be hungry when you didn't even eat lunch?"

"I'm just not."

"Fine." I opened a lower cabinet with my foot and took out a bag of pretzels. "You want a soda?" I asked.

"No."

I sighed and hoped he didn't die of dehydration—it was still in the nineties outside.

We made our way to the small living room, where Connor spotted my guitar in the corner. "Is that your guitar?"

"Yep," I said, opening the TV cabinet with my foot.

"Will you play for me? I can't wait to see you play it with your feet."

"Maybe another day. I'm kind of out of practice right now." That wasn't exactly true. I felt shy about it, like I needed to prepare before I performed for him—if I ever would perform for him. I still hadn't made up my mind.

"Promise?" Connor said.

"I'll play for you sometime. Just not right now."

Connor turned his attention to the row of video games in the cabinet. "You have some good ones in here," he said, thumbing through them.

"My dad likes to play. They're mostly his games."

"Your dad's cool," Connor said, clearly impressed by my dad's immaturity. He pulled out an ultraviolent war game. "Let's play this."

I shook my head. "Not allowed. For Dad only."

Connor frowned, put the game back in the cabinet, and pulled out another game I wasn't allowed to play. "I'm not allowed to play any game with a disclaimer on the cover," I said. I walked to the cabinet and pulled out a racing game. "Let's play this one."

"I guess." Connor let out a dramatic sigh, clearly disappointed we wouldn't get to battle each other to our bloody virtual deaths.

"I'm better at games when I can mostly use the joy stick," I said as Connor slipped the disc into the console.

"That's good because you'll need every advantage to beat me."

We played for a couple of hours. I don't think Connor expected me to be such a good player. Yeah, he did beat me a lot, but I gave him a good fight and even won a couple of races myself. I think I played worse than normal because Connor ticced a lot while he played, and it distracted me. I guess the tics probably made it harder for him to play, as well. I thought about him at home playing video games all night by himself, ticcing badly. Maybe it wasn't good for him to spend all his free time doing that.

I felt like I was starting to understand Connor's tics—what made them worse and what made them better. Definitely when Connor was stressed or excited about anything, his tics got worse. When he felt calm and comfortable, they weren't so bad. I guess video games got him worked up.

Mom walked in the door just as we were putting the games away. "You absolutely would not believe what Bob did now," she said as she threw her hat down on the kitchen table.

I looked at Connor and whispered (in a Dracula accent for some reason), "Murdered someone." He giggled.

She walked into the living room and saw Connor. "This must be Connor." She reached out her hand to shake with his.

"Nice to meet you, Mrs. Green," Connor said softly. I could tell he was trying to hold his tics in.

"Nice to meet you, too," Mom said.

Connor let out a loud bark and Mom jumped back. "Oh, my." She giggled. "That was interesting."

"Connor has Tourette syndrome," I reminded her.

"Oh," she said. "That's right. Don't look so nervous, honey." Mom touched Connor's arm to put him at ease. "It will only make your tics worse."

I looked at her in surprise. "Mom, you know about Tourette's?"

She gave me an annoyed look. "Aven, I was a psych major in college. Of course I know about Tourette's."

"You were a psych major in college?" I said. "What's that?"

She sighed and rolled her eyes. "Psychology. Don't you ever listen to me when I talk?"

"No," I joked, "'cause you usually just talk about boring old people stuff."

Mom grabbed me and ran her knuckles over my head, messing up my hair. "Ouch!" I cried, wriggling away from her.

"All right, I'm going to get dinner started. Will you two do me a favor and run over to the gold mine and fire Bob?"

I smiled, but Connor looked grave. "Thank you, Mrs. Green, but I'm not staying for dinner."

"Yes, you are," I said. "Your mom's working. What are you going to eat for dinner if you don't eat with us?"

Connor froze up, like he had no idea what to say to that. "I'll eat . . . cereal."

"That's unacceptable," Mom said. "You're eating with us. Then I'll take you home after dinner since your mom's working."

Connor appeared absolutely terrified at the thought. "No . . . really . . . I like . . . cereal." He could barely get the words out from his ticcing.

"Why won't you eat, Connor?" I asked. "Are you anorexic?"

He seemed to relax a little at that and laughed. "No, I'm not anorexic. I just . . ."

"What?" I nearly shouted. "I'm your friend, Connor. Tell me."

"Sometimes I . . . spit when I eat." Connor's cheeks

were bright red as he shrugged and blinked his eyes rapidly. "I spit food at people."

Mom gave Connor an understanding smile. "That's not uncommon," she said. "We'll all wear rain gear at dinner tonight." And with that, she opened a cabinet and started pulling out potatoes.

Connor looked at me. "I hope you have face masks, too."

I kicked at his shoe. "See? It's no big deal. We know you can't help it."

Connor's expression changed. "I wish my parents were as understanding as yours. It got to the point at home that neither one of them wanted to eat with me anymore. My dad would yell at me for spitting and that would make it worse." He tugged at his hair. "Now I just eat in my room by myself. My mom's hardly ever around so it doesn't matter anyway."

"It matters," I said emphatically. "It matters a lot."

As we were setting the table for dinner, Dad walked in. "I think that old llama might have to be put down," he said sadly, shoulders slumped.

My head shot up. "What? No, not Spaghetti!" I cried. Mom and Dad both gave me a funny look. I shrugged. "We have a special connection." I looked at Connor. "We're X-Men," I added softly.

"I'm sorry, honey," Dad said. "He's so old. He's like twenty-two years old. Denise said he's hardly eaten in two days. And that thing growing out of his head—well, it can't be comfortable."

"I'll nurse him back to health," I insisted.

"I'm not sure that's possible at his age," Dad said. "Anyway, we can talk about it later. The vet's coming tomorrow, and we'll see how he does over the next few days."

By the time we all sat down at the table together, I didn't have much appetite. I kept thinking about poor Spaghetti not being able to eat. I looked at Connor. I could tell he was hesitant to take a bite of his pork chop.

"It's okay, Connor," Dad said. "We're all prepared." Dad lifted something off his lap: ski goggles. He slipped them over his eyes. "No worries."

"David!" Mom cried, punching Dad in the arm. "That's terrible."

Connor laughed, though. It seemed to put him at ease, and he finally took a bite of his mashed potatoes.

"Don't worry," Mom said. "Everything is non-staining."

I glared at Dad. "All the things we had to get rid of, and you brought *ski goggles* with us to Arizona."

"These were like eighty bucks," he defended himself.

"So, Connor," Dad said, removing his ridiculous goggles, "what are you interested in? I mean besides pulling morbid pranks with my daughter and scaring our visitors away." Dad narrowed his eyes at me. "You might want to rethink hanging out with her—she's a bad influence."

"And you have terrible sideburns," I said, unable to come up with anything better. He really did have bad sideburns—they were horribly uneven.

Dad ignored me. "So?" he said, returning his attention to Connor.

"Uh, I like movies," Connor said. "I have a huge movie collection at home."

"Oh, why don't I take you guys to the movies this weekend?" Mom said, clearly thrilled I had made a friend.

Connor looked appalled and shrunk down in his seat. He shook his head rapidly. "No, no. No movie theaters."

"You don't go to the movies?" I said.

"No way. I went only once since my tics started a few years ago, and it was *not* a fun experience."

"What happened?" I asked.

"People complained, of course. No one wants to listen to a dog barking while they try to watch a movie."

"That's messed up," I said. "People are so rude."

"They're not rude," Connor said. "They don't know I have Tourette's. That's what makes it so embarrassing."

I scrunched up my nose. "You should wear a T-shirt that says 'I have Tourette's' on it everywhere you go. Then people will leave you alone."

Connor snorted. "Yeah, maybe you could make me one, Aven."

Then he kicked my foot under the table gently. "Should we tell them?" he whispered.

"Tell us what?" Mom said.

I gave my parents a highly serious look. "We think there may be a murderer at Stagecoach Pass."

Dad coughed and choked on his mouthful of pork chop. Mom slapped him on the back while he hacked his food into his napkin. When he could finally breathe, he gasped, "What? Why would you think such a thing?"

We updated Mom and Dad on our theories about the Cavanaughs.

"Aven," Mom said. "Just because people are secretive doesn't mean they've been murdered."

"I have to admit, Sheebs," Dad said, "you haven't exactly presented us with the most convincing evidence."

"Some people just really value their privacy," Mom added.

I nodded at them like I agreed, but Connor and I gave each other knowing looks. Yeah, right—like we were going to let it go that easily.

Then Connor looked from me to my parents and back again. "So where does Aven get her red hair from?" he asked.

"I'm adopted, Connor," I said.

"Oh, that's cool," said Connor.

"It's so cool," said Mom.

I rolled my eyes. "Here she goes. She loves telling people about my adoption."

Connor looked at Mom with interest, so she took that as her cue to tell the story for the millionth time. "Well," she began, "Aven's dad and I couldn't have a baby, so we figured we'd end up adopting one. I started reading a lot about adoption online. Then one day I was on this website and there was a tab that said 'Kids in need of a forever family,' so I clicked on it. I scrolled down until I saw it—the most precious little angel baby face I'd ever seen in my entire life."

"It was mine, in case you were wondering," I said.

"I knew the moment I saw her she was my daughter," Mom went on. "With those chubby pink cheeks and bright red mop of hair."

"She'd never seen such a precious, beautiful, amazing,

brilliant, intelligent child," I said. Connor raised an eyebrow at me. "I may be embellishing a little."

"No, she's not at all," Mom said. "I knew right at the moment I saw her that I was looking into the face of my daughter. It was like she was born for me right in that moment. Some women birth babies through their you-know-whats, but I birthed Aven through the computer that day."

I groaned. "Mom, that is the *worst* part of your story. Connor totally didn't need to hear that."

"Really, Laura," Dad said. "It's the worst. It's just awful."

She glared at Dad before returning to her story. "Anyway, right below her picture it said, 'Aven, two years old.' I couldn't believe she was two years old and hadn't been adopted yet."

"Yeah, she didn't realize she was on an adoption website for children with special needs," I said.

"So I clicked on her picture and that's when I saw she didn't have arms."

"And it didn't even matter," I said. "She wanted me anyway."

Mom gave me her gushy love face. "So I broke the news to her dad that night at dinner."

"Yeah," Dad said. "She told me my future daughter

was a beautiful redhead. Oh, and also that she didn't have arms."

"How did you feel about it?" Connor asked.

"Well, you know, I was surprised, of course, but once I saw her I agreed wholeheartedly—she was our daughter." Dad gave me his own version of the gushy love face.

"We did a lot of research before we got Aven so we could give her the best care," Mom said. "You know, Connor, there are a lot of amazing people in the world who don't have arms."

"Really?" said Connor.

"Yes," said Mom. "There's a successful architect who designs skyscrapers by using his feet to type, just like Aven does on her computer, and a woman who paints beautiful artwork that sells for quite a bit of money."

"There's that guy who's the motivational speaker," Dad added.

"Oh, yeah," Mom said. "And then there are people just living totally regular lives, raising babies and driving cars and doing everything people with arms do."

"That's so cool," said Connor.

"Remember when we visited that teacher? What was his name? Carl?" Dad said to Mom.

"We found him through his website," Mom told

Connor. "It was called Unarmed Education. We had to drive all the way to Colorado to meet him, but it was so worth it."

"He showed us how he did all kinds of things," Dad said. "He even drove us to the grocery store."

"Yeah." Mom laughed. "David chewed his fingernails the whole way there."

"Can you blame me?" Dad asked Connor.

"Anyway," Mom said. "He shopped for food all on his own and made us a lovely dinner with his feet. We knew Aven would be able to do all these things and more. When we finally got her, though, she couldn't do anything." Mom threw her arms up in exasperation. "Her foster families had done everything for her—bathed her, fed her, brushed her teeth. She just sat around like a slug, waiting to be cared for like the Queen of Sheba."

"Queen. Of. Sheba," Dad reiterated. "Or Sheebs, for short."

I rolled my eyes. "And this was when Mom's full-time job became teaching Aven how to do stuff."

"Right away," Mom said, "I was dumping out jars of marbles and telling her to put them all back in the jar, giving her a bowl of fish crackers and telling her to feed them to herself one at a time, giving her a sheet of stickers and a blank piece of paper and telling her to decorate it, telling her to brush her own teeth, wash her own feet, scratch her own itches."

"Come to think of it," I said. "It wasn't so much teaching me how to do stuff as it was telling me to do stuff."

"That may be," Mom said. "But mostly it was telling her she could do just about anything if she tried hard enough."

"Yeah, I got over being the Queen of Sheba pretty quickly," I said.

"I can see that," said Connor, and with that he spit his mouthful of mashed potatoes right in my face.

"HEY," I SAID, WALKING UP TO Connor a couple of days later at his locker.

He turned around to face me. "Hey. How's Spaghetti?"

"Better." I had spent as much time with him as I could, trying to motivate him to get well and eat his hay, even offering it to him with my feet. I also made sure he ate his llama ration. My efforts seemed to be working.

"That's good," Connor said. "Do you know why he's named Spaghetti? Seems like a weird name for a llama."

"Denise told me he's named after spaghetti westerns."

"Oh," Connor said. "What are those?"

I shrugged. "No idea. Maybe movies full of cowboys eating lots of spaghetti."

Connor nodded. "Weird."

I saw Zion walking down the sidewalk toward us. "Hey, Zion," I called to him. He was concentrating so hard on watching his feet, he didn't hear me. "Zion!" I called again.

He looked up, seemingly surprised again that someone was talking to him. I can't exactly wave to get someone's attention, so I jumped up and down a little bit. "Zion," I said again as I bounced. He finally saw me.

He stopped in front of me and Connor. "Hi, Aven," he said softly.

"This is Connor," I told him, and the two boys gave each other a little mini-wave.

"You're in my history class," Zion told Connor. "I've, uh, heard you in there."

Connor barked and shrugged his shoulders. "You and everyone else."

"Connor has Tourette syndrome," I explained to Zion. "He can't help it."

"Oh. I didn't think he could." Zion looked down at his sneakers, then back up at Connor. "I'm sorry."

Connor shrugged again. "It's okay."

"Anyway," I said, "I was just about to ask Connor if he wanted to come over after school and do some investigating." I eyed Zion seriously. "I live at this theme park called Stagecoach Pass—"

"Yeah, I know that place," said Zion.

"Oh, good," I said. "We're trying to figure out why no one ever sees the owner. We think he might have even been . . ." I looked around and whispered, "*murdered*."

Zion took a step back. "That sounds scary."

Connor barked. "Trust me, there's nothing scary about that place."

"I don't know about that," I said. "This morning, when I left the apartment, I found a dead lizard right at the bottom of the stairs." I sighed and nodded. "Yep. I think someone was trying to send me a message."

"What kind of message?" Zion asked.

"Stop butting your nose in where it doesn't belong, or I'll send you some dead lizards," I said. "Obviously."

Connor shook his head. "I don't know. Stuff dies in the desert all the time. That's kind of what the desert does—kills stuff."

"Well, you guys should come over. I'll show you the dead lizard and we can search the storage shed more."

Connor slammed his locker shut. "I can't. My mom needs me to wait at home for the maintenance guy. For some reason our hot water won't work."

"Oh, that stinks," I said.

"I can't either," said Zion. "And I'm not sure I want

to get involved with murders and dead lizards and stuff. I don't know if my parents would like it."

"It's only *one* murder and *one* dead lizard." I rolled my eyes and tapped my foot. "How about tomorrow? It's Saturday."

"Yeah," Connor said. "I can come over early."

We both looked at Zion. "Okay," he said. "But if anyone sends you any more dead animals, I'm out."

"Great," I said. "I can't wait for tomorrow."

As Connor, Zion, and I walked together down the sidewalk, I heard someone do that coughing thing when they sneak a word into the cough, but they're not actually being very sneaky about it at all.

And the word was *freaks*.

THE NEXT MORNING, I WROTE A
new blog post.

> I'm sure most people who see me feel sorry for
> me at first. I think their first thought is probably
> something about how terrible it must be to not
> have arms. Maybe they imagine me helplessly
> being carried around by my mom everywhere in a
> giant baby backpack and my poor parents having
> to brush my teeth and feed me through a tube
> and change my diapers and whatever.
>
> What a lot of people don't realize, though, is there
> are a lot of fantastic things about not having arms.

Seriously, I can think of twenty right now:

1.   No fistfighting. This is really a positive for other people because I would totally win in any fistfight. No really, it would be a total smackdown.

2.   No rough elbows. My mom has eczema, so I know what a curse rough elbows can be.

3.   No need to clean my fingernails. You can add filing, polishing, and trimming to that as well.

4.   No leaving fingerprints behind at a crime scene—very helpful if I ever rob a bank.

5.   No getting caught picking my nose. My shoes are usually in the way.

6.   No arm wrestling.

7.   No golf. Well, I suppose I could figure out a way to play golf but I'm so not gonna because golf is booooring.

8. No cheesy high fives.

9. No making that silly okay! circle shape with my fingers.

10. Fewer areas to put sunscreen on and fewer areas to sunburn. This is a good thing for me because I have super-fair skin.

11. I don't have to worry about accidentally using my hands in soccer. I guess that gives me an advantage.

12. No fighting over the arm rest at the movies. Really, no fighting over the arm rest anywhere.

13. No arm pits. How can there be pits when there are no arms? They're more like . . . flats.

14. I'll get the royal treatment when I start driving in a few years. That's right—it's princess-parking for this girl everywhere I go. And, yes, I will be driving an actual car. Watch out, roads!

15. Less money spent on jewelry—rings, bracelets, watches, etc.

16. No flabby flapjack arms when I get old. My great-grandma has those. Hopefully she's not reading this.

17. No push-ups.

18. I never get that floppy, numb arm thing at night from sleeping on my arms. My dad gets that just about every night.

19. No one's ever challenged me to a thumb war. Which is good. Because I don't like war.

20. Pranks that work. One day I'll pull a fantastic prank like pretending my arms get torn off in an elevator door or something. I look forward to that.

I stared at the screen. Who exactly was I trying to convince? The person who'd called me a freak yesterday? Or myself? I hit Publish and browsed through some of my previous posts. I noticed that Emily had commented on a lot of them—mostly short remarks like "LOL!" or "Miss you, girl!" Someone else had commented that I was in their art class at school, though they didn't say who they were. A couple of other people wrote that I made them laugh. That was nice.

I was responding to one of Emily's comments when I heard a knock at the door. I let Connor in, and we played video games while we waited for Zion to show.

When we heard another knock, I jumped up and opened the door. Zion stood there, looking all shy as usual, with his mom. She had the biggest smile I had ever seen. "I just wanted to meet these new friends of Zion's," she said. She looked like she might explode from happiness. I guessed from her expression she didn't meet a lot of his friends. I remembered what Zion had said about his parents being huge geeks as I took in her Wolverine tank top and purple skirt. I thought she looked pretty cool.

"Hi." I resisted the urge to stare at my own feet like Zion. "I'm Aven." I turned and looked at Connor. "That's Connor." Connor barked as he continued playing the game, totally ignoring us.

"I'm Zion's mom," she said. She wore a sparkly purple headband in her curly black hair. I wanted one of those sparkly purple headbands. And the matching purple skirt.

She looked at me with eyes that were the same exact deep brown as Zion's. "What game are you guys playing?" she asked.

"Just Mario Kart," I said.

She glanced from Connor to me and back again, and for one terrifying moment I thought she was going to ask if she could play with us. Instead, she looked down at Zion. "Well, have fun playing with your new friends, sweetie pie," she said and kissed him on top of his head.

Zion groaned a little. "You can go now, Mom," he said, but not really in a mean way.

She turned that beaming smile back on me. "I'll be back in a few hours if that's okay."

"Okay," I said.

When I shut the door, Zion sighed and said, "I thought she would *never* leave," even though she'd only been standing there for about one minute.

"Hey, where'd your mom get her headband?" I asked Zion.

He looked at me like I was crazy. "I don't know."

We played a couple more races, and then I led the two guys to the storage shed.

Connor rummaged through the junk while Zion and I tried to read some old documents we found stacked in a giant heap in one corner. Periodically Connor would hold something up for us like an old boot or a handkerchief and say, "Check this out," like whatever he was holding was interesting, when, in fact, it was not.

Connor also found an entire box of books about tarantulas. "Cool," I said, dipping my toes into the box and sifting through the books. "Maybe you guys can carry this up to the apartment for me."

While I browsed through one of the tarantula books, Zion continued moving the stacks of documents and boxes until he uncovered a large wooden desk buried beneath all the stuff. Connor and I examined the desk with him—it had a row of drawers going down one side, but those were locked. "Where do you think the key is?" Zion asked me.

I shrugged. "This desk is probably like fifty years old. It could be anywhere. You know how to pry it open?"

Zion shook his head. "It's so dusty in here." He coughed. "And my mom's going to be back soon."

I sighed. "Yeah, I guess we can give up for today."

"Wait, look," Connor said. He reached under the desk and pulled out an old guitar. It was pretty beaten-up from neglect and the strings were missing. On the back of it, in very small letters, someone had carved the initials A. B. C.

"What do you think they stand for?" Connor asked. "The alphabet?"

"No." I ran a toe over the carved letters. "Something, something, Cavanaugh."

17

"SO, LIKE, I KNOW YOU DON'T go to therapy anymore and all that, but my mom and I were browsing online, and we found out there's this, uh . . . social event for kids with Tourette's over at the hospital," I said, walking next to Connor on our way to class the following week.

Connor stopped and turned to face me. "You mean a support group."

"Well, sort of," I said.

"I don't need a support group. I'm totally fine."

"I just thought it would be cool to meet some other kids who have the same thing as you, you know? Maybe even make some new friends." Actually, it had mostly been Mom's idea, but she thought it would be best if I brought it up so Connor would be more open to it.

Connor raised an eyebrow at me. "I don't know."

"It would be just as much for me as you," I said. "It turns out I like kids who have Tourette's, and I don't have all that many friends. So I'd like to go and see about making some new friends in a place where I'm not the only kid who's sort of different."

Connor continued giving me his skeptical look. "Really?"

"Well, I looked up support groups for kids with no arms, and guess what? There are none. At least not that I could find. I guess Tourette's is a lot more common."

"One percent," Connor said as he turned and continued walking toward class.

"What?"

"One percent of people have Tourette's."

"See!" I blurted. "I bet lots of kids with Tourette's go to this social event."

"Support group."

"Whatever. It might be fine. Please will you go with me? Please?" I begged.

"Are you saying you'd go without me?" he asked.

"Why not?"

"Uh, because you don't have Tourette's."

"Well, I could just meow from time to time. No one would know."

Connor gave me a playful shove. "Fine, I'll go with you." He rolled his eyes. "And you won't have to meow."

Mom walked us into the hospital just after seven-thirty. A receptionist directed us down a corridor and into a small meeting room. Mom promised to pick us up in front of the hospital at nine o'clock sharp and left us there to brave the meeting alone.

As we entered the room, we were immediately greeted by a boy shouting, "Chicken nipple!"

I looked at him in surprise, and he shouted it again, aiming it at no one in particular. I glanced at the other kids in the room—five boys and only one other girl. "What's with all the boys?" I whispered in Connor's ear.

"Tourette's is way more common for boys." Connor barked as we stood there surveying the room. The other kids didn't seem at all fazed by his barking, but they watched me with curiosity. That was okay.

A pretty woman walked into the room and introduced herself to us. "I'm Andrea," she said, shaking Connor's hand. "Are you Connor?"

Connor nodded, barked, shrugged, blinked his eyes. He was nervous. I could tell.

"And you're Aven, Connor's friend?" Andrea said.

"Nice to meet you," I said.

"Why don't you two find a place to sit and we'll get started." I could see Andrea also had Tourette's by the way she made a funny counting motion with her fingers, but other than that, she seemed to keep it under control. I wondered if she had a milder form of Tourette's or if she had learned how to control it—if so, I wanted to find out how for Connor.

Chicken Nipple Boy moved over a seat so Connor and I could sit next to each other. He yelled out, "Chicken nipple!" as I sat down next to him, then he leaned over and whispered to me, "Do you have Tourette's?"

I shook my head. "No."

"Oh. Chicken nipple. I do, in case you—chicken nipple—didn't notice."

I grinned at him. "I wasn't really sure."

"I'm Dexter," he said. "Chicken nipple."

"I'm Aven."

"Well," Andrea said, sitting down at the circle. "I guess we can get started. Everyone, we have a couple of new friends with us tonight." She turned to us. "Why don't you guys introduce yourselves?"

Connor was ticcing badly, so I spoke. "I'm Aven."

"Aven doesn't have Tourette's," Andrea said.

"Yeah." I laughed. "Can you imagine? What a doozy that would be."

Dexter laughed out loud and shouted, "Chicken nipple!" and the other kids softly chuckled a bit. I liked Dexter already.

"At least if you had Tourette's," the completely monotone, expressionless girl sitting across from me said, "you wouldn't have to worry about slapping yourself in the face all the time like I do." As though on cue, the girl slapped herself in the face.

"Yeah, but you should see what Aven can do with her feet," Connor said, blinking his eyes rapidly. "Face-slapping isn't that far-fetched."

"I want to—chicken nipple—see what you can do with your feet," Dexter said.

"Maybe later if we have time and Aven doesn't mind," Andrea said, smiling. She clearly enjoyed the lighthearted conversation among us kids, and honestly, so did I. Andrea turned her attention to Connor. "Introduce yourself, Connor."

"I'm Connor. I do have Tourette's. As if you couldn't tell." He barked.

"Well, welcome, you two," Andrea said. "We're so happy to have you. Why don't we all go around and introduce ourselves? We'll start with you, Dexter."

"Chicken nipple. I'm Dexter. And as you can see, I love to say *chicken nipple*. Chicken nipple."

Connor gaped at Dexter. "I have to know—why chicken nipple? Why not another word?"

"Dexter has a rarer form of Tourette's called coprolalia," Andrea explained. "He says words and phrases, some of which people may find inappropriate, but he can't help it."

Connor turned his attention back to Dexter. "Yeah, but why chicken nipple?"

Dexter laughed. "Sometimes I say other—chicken nipple—things. I'm glad when it's just chicken nipple. Chicken nipple. Sometimes I say 'barbecue' or 'pirate ship' or 'I love bubble baths' and some—chicken nipple—other things. Sometimes I say my own name, which is really embarrassing for some reason.

"One time I went through a short period—chicken nipple—when I said, 'I'll punch a baby' every time I saw a baby. That was awful. Chicken nipple. People would run away from me with their—chicken nipple—babies." Dexter looked at me with a straight face. "Chicken nipple. I swear I would never punch a baby. I like babies."

"I believe you," I said, trying to maintain a straight face myself.

Just then Dexter cried out, "Barbecue chicken sandwiches," and everyone laughed, especially Dexter. I normally would never in a million years laugh at someone's disability, but I realized we were all laughing with Dexter, certainly not at him. And it was okay. I think it made everyone feel better in a way.

Josh introduced himself next. Josh made the same whooping sound all the time and had what Andrea explained were several motor tics. This included bending over a lot and sort of like playing air guitar. Other than that, Josh was quiet.

The girl introduced herself as Rebecca. I already knew Rebecca slapped herself in the face. She even wore little padded gloves to help soften the blows. I had never realized Tourette's could be painful, even damaging to the person who had it. Rebecca also grunted and coughed a lot, even though she didn't have a cold or anything.

Jack rolled his eyes constantly and shook his head. He also made a strange yelling sound like nothing I had ever heard—like he sucked in air so fast it made a shrieking sound.

Zachary rolled his shoulders so much, he feared he would need surgery on his already worn down fifteen-year-old joints.

Mason made constant farting noises with his mouth and pulled on his hair, which made his hair patchy because he pulled on it so much that some of it would come out at times. Mason had over fifty tics, he told us. I couldn't imagine having to deal with that many uncontrollable things going on in my body. Besides Dexter, Mason's tics were probably the most embarrassing of the group. He hardly ever went out in public—like Connor.

Andrea guided us into a discussion on how we felt about going out in public—more specifically, going places like the movies, library, etc. Connor wasn't alone in not liking to go to the movies—no one ever really went. Rebecca was the only one who felt okay going to most places because her vocal tics weren't as loud as the others and could almost sound normal at times if you assumed she had a bad cough or something. People still got annoyed by her frequently, though.

As cool as Dexter was, he was terrified of going out in public. I guess he said "I'll punch a baby" in front of some dad holding a baby in the drugstore one day, and the dad nearly attacked him. Had Dexter's mom not intervened, it could have been bad. Once again, I thought if he had been wearing a T-shirt explaining he had Tourette's, maybe the situation could have been avoided.

Dexter also had obsessive-compulsive disorder, which Andrea explained often accompanied Tourette's. It was hard for him to leave the house because he worried so much that the stove and oven were on at home. He even asked if he could call his mom a couple of times during the meeting so he could have her check them. Andrea let him.

It sounded as though most everyone's parents were supportive and understanding of their Tourette's. Well, everyone except Connor's parents. Some of their extended family members, such as aunts, uncles, and grandparents, often accused them of faking it for attention, like Connor's dad did. I thought it would be exhausting to put on such an act all the time. I couldn't fathom why anyone would want to do such a thing or how anyone could think they were doing it.

It was strange listening to everyone speak among a cacophony of barking, farting, whooping, shrieking, and chicken nipples. It was also strangely comforting. No one cared about my lack of arms; they were all far too caught up in their own struggles. And I, for once, felt completely normal among this group of misfits. I hoped Connor felt the same way and would come back with me again.

"So how was the meeting?" Mom asked as she drove us home.

"It was great." I looked at Connor for confirmation.

"Yeah," Connor said. "It was really good." He looked out the window.

"That's great. What did you guys talk about?"

"All kinds of stuff," I said. "Like what everyone's tics were and how they felt about going out in public and things like that."

I could see Mom watching Connor in the rearview mirror. "Do you think it was helpful, Connor?"

"Hmm?" he said absentmindedly.

"I asked if you thought it was helpful," Mom said again.

Connor shrugged. "I guess so. Yeah, it was nice to meet other kids like me. I just . . ."

"What?" I asked when Connor trailed off.

"I'm worried I'll start swearing like Dexter."

"I don't really think of 'chicken nipple' as a swear word," I said.

"You know what I mean."

"You heard Andrea," I said. "That's pretty rare."

"Yeah, but Dexter started out like me, too—making strange noises and movements. And then one day he said 'chicken nipple,' and everything changed. I guess I'm afraid the same thing will happen to me." I couldn't see Connor's face as he gazed out his window. "Things are hard enough the way they are. I can't imagine how hard it would be if I started saying obnoxious things all the time. I think I'd *rather* have brain surgery at that point."

"You shouldn't worry about it," I said. "I think the more you worry about it and stress yourself out, the worse your tics will be. And maybe if you start saying words, it will just be normal stuff, like 'I love African safaris' or something like that."

Connor chuckled. "That's normal?"

"Yes, for someone who loves African safaris. I don't think you should think about it too much."

"When's the next meeting?" Mom asked, obviously trying to change the subject.

"Next month," I said. "They meet once a month. We should go back because we're going to talk about relaxation and how it can help when we're out in public."

"You mean when *we're* out in public," Connor said. "You don't have to worry about that stuff, Aven."

"Maybe not that kind of stuff. I may not have tics, but I still have to deal with people staring at me and treating me like I'm different."

"Yeah, but you don't call attention to yourself. I think I'd give up my arms to get rid of my Tourette's."

"Don't say that," I said. "I like you just the way you are."

"Really?" Connor gave me a skeptical look.

"Yep. Tics and all."

BY LATE FALL, THE WEATHER WAS finally starting to cool down to a comfortable temperature. I had read every single tarantula book from the Desert Ridge Middle School library, the Phoenix Library, and the box we'd found in the storage shed. I now knew terrifying things about tarantulas—like that a type of wasp called a tarantula hawk would sting and paralyze a tarantula, then lay its egg on it and seal the tarantula up in a burrow. Once the wasp grub hatched, it would feed on the tarantula meat. *Gack*. I couldn't wait to use that information to shock someone—I even blogged about it.

I had written several more posts on my blog—mostly stuff about the park, school, tarantulas, and how I do things without arms. Pretty random stuff—so

I called my blog *Aven's Random Thoughts*. Anyway, it wasn't about anything terribly exciting, but I had gained a few more followers. Zion now commented pretty regularly on my posts, and Emily still made her usual "LOL" and "I miss you" remarks from time to time, though I hadn't seen any comments from my other friends in Kansas for at least a week.

Dad and I practiced soccer in the arena together early on weekend mornings when it was cool outside. It was wonderful to feel a chill in the air again, but every weekend I felt less and less enthusiastic about getting out of bed to go out there. I think Dad must have noticed my waning interest. He found an old tuba somewhere at the park, and he came into my room one morning, played horrible screeching sounds on the tuba, then announced, "All hail Aven Laura Green, future queen of the Desert Ridge Middle School soccer team!" I smothered my face with a pillow and told him there was no such thing as a queen in soccer. The next weekend he played the tuba and announced, "All hail Aven Laura Green, future emperor of the Desert Ridge Middle School soccer team!" And the weekend after that: "All hail Aven Laura Green, future world dictator of the Desert Ridge Middle School soccer team!"

Dad said the snakes would be hibernating now,

so after we practiced soccer, I would hike up the hill behind Stagecoach Pass. I liked being able to look down on the park and the rest of the city, and I liked visiting my giant saguaro.

I spent most of the time on the hill looking for tarantulas and collecting quartz rocks (I had quite the collection going at home). I wore a loose, open bag around my neck so I could easily drop the rocks in with my toes.

Most of the kids at school were now ignoring me completely. I guess they were used to seeing me around by now, so I wasn't getting any more shocked looks. It was more like I just didn't exist.

I sat next to my giant saguaro awhile looking down at poor old Billy and Fred, endlessly hauling kids around the dirt trail. I thought it might be time for them to retire to the petting zoo. I wondered if we could replace them with a little train like one I had seen in a mall.

Now that the weather was cooling down, business had picked up a bit, but my parents told me it was barely enough to keep the park running and cover all the repairs that were building up.

I stood and walked around to the back side of the hill, hoping to find some new rocks. A strand of something dark caught my eye. I slipped my foot out of my flat, grabbed it with my toes, and tried to pick it up. It was connected to something in the ground and wouldn't come loose. I put my flat back on and started kicking at the dirt, trying to unearth whatever was under there.

Eventually, I loosened enough dirt to get the strand free. I laid it out on the ground and studied it—it was caked with dirt, but I could tell it had once been a necklace with a polished turquoise stone set into a dark metal. I lifted it with my toes and slipped it into my bag. I rushed home to call Connor and tell him what I'd found. After all, we'd seen that necklace before.

CONNOR, ZION, AND I SAT OUTSIDE

on the lawn together before school, waiting for the first bell to ring. Connor studied the necklace while Zion flipped gently through the fragile sketchbook. Every now and then a brittle piece of paper would flake off, and we'd all gasp. Zion finally found the page that had the sketch of the necklace. "That's definitely it," he said.

Connor held the necklace up. "The metal is nearly black and in the sketch it's light gray."

"My mom told me that's because it's tarnished silver," I said. "Look at the shape of the stone and that little vein running through it. It's definitely the same."

"But why was it up on the hill?" Connor asked, then barked.

I shrugged. "I have no idea."

Zion looked from me to Connor and back again, his eyes huge with alarm. "What?" I asked him. He covered his mouth and shook his head, like what he was thinking was too terrible to say. "What?" I said again.

"Dead body," Zion whispered.

Connor and I looked at each other. "I don't know," I said.

"What other explanation could there be?" said Zion. "Someone murdered this necklace-wearing person and buried her body up on the hill. Why else would it be up there?"

Connor looked at me wide-eyed. "Rodeo clown mafia," he said and snickered.

I shook my head at him and tried to remain serious. "I spend a lot of time up on that hill, and I've never seen any sign of a grave or anything."

"It could have happened a long time ago," Zion said. "Maybe bushes and cactuses and stuff have grown over it. I've heard a dead body makes good fertilizer."

Connor and I laughed. "That's so gross," I said. "Where could you have possibly heard that?"

Zion scratched at his chin. "I think I read it in a comic book."

"Oh, then it's definitely true," I said. Zion tore a

handful of grass out of the ground and threw it at me. I shook my hair out. "I guess there could be a dead body up there, but you'd think I'd feel all creepy when I was up there if there was. Like I'd feel a chill or a shudder or a . . ." I thought for a moment. "Or a tremble!"

Connor smiled and barked. Then, almost immediately, we heard another bark from a nearby crowd.

Connor's face dropped. I turned and glared at the group of kids standing near us. Several of them were covering their smiles with their hands as they snuck glances at us.

I turned back to Connor. "You shouldn't put up with that."

Connor's shoulders slumped. "What am I supposed to do about it?"

Normally, I would never want to call attention to myself. But there are times when my temper overwhelms my desire to go unnoticed.

I stood up and shouted at the group, "Whoever's doing that, it's not nice! You should be ashamed of yourself!"

I sat back down on the ground with a "humph!" Connor and Zion looked shocked at my behavior. "There," I said. "That's what you should do."

CONNOR AND I ATE LUNCH WITH

Zion behind the office most days now. Connor still hardly ate anything, but he took a bite from time to time. Sometimes he'd spit his food, but he always tried to aim at the brick wall. Every now and then, though, Zion and I would have to do some serious ninja blocks when a pretzel or grape flew at our heads.

I sat with the boys on the sidewalk by the office as Zion said, "I think I might audition for *The Wizard of Oz.*" He blushed so hard, I could see the red coloring his brown cheeks.

"Oh yeah, what part?" I asked him.

He shrugged. "I dunno."

I thought for a moment. "You would make a good . . . lion."

He frowned. "Because I'm so fat."

"No, because you need to find your courage." I nudged him with my foot. "I'm only half serious."

He smiled. "Have you guys ever done anything like that?"

"What? Auditioned for a play?" Connor asked

"Yeah."

Connor looked at Zion like he was crazy. "Yeah, right," he said.

I frowned at Connor. "You'd probably be a good actor," I said.

"The only part I could ever play," Connor said to me, "would be the part of an annoying, yappy dog."

I didn't know what else to say about that, so I told them, "My school back in Kansas held this playwright contest in sixth grade. Anyone could submit their own ideas, plot, and script for a play. The winner got to have their play produced. I submitted the most awesome script of all time. Wait for it," I said dramatically. "*Down and Dirty in Kansas City.*"

Zion snorted and a little of his juice box came out his nose. He wiped it away. "What was *that* about?"

I cleared my throat. "*Down and Dirty in Kansas City* is the story of a completely awesome ninja named Harold who lives in Kansas City and fights criminals with the help of his trusty pig named Jerold. So Harold and Jerold are this crime-fighting duo who stop a gang of criminals from robbing a bank. They also fall in love. Not with each other. With a beautiful vixen lady and a lady pig. The play ends in a double-wedding for Harold and Jerold and their partners."

Connor giggled and Zion choked on a little more juice box.

"The climax of the play," I continued, "was supposed to be when Harold and Jerold finally face off with the main villain," I tossed my hair back, "played by me. And the exciting battle to the death ends in Harold and Jerold ripping my arms off and blood splattering everywhere while I drop dead to the floor." I had thought we could borrow those fake arms again from Emily's mom.

"Did you win?" Zion asked.

"I *totally* didn't win. Plus we had to have a meeting with my parents. They had read my play already and thought it rocked, so they were a little confused about the whole thing. I tuned out most of the meeting, but I believe the words *gruesome* and *horrifying* may have been said.

"Anyway, this kid named Luke won the contest. His play was called *Desert Moon over the Desert*. I found the title redundant, but I guess the judges thought his work was spectacularly creative. What can you expect from the same people who thought *Down and Dirty in Kansas City* was a stinker?"

"Really," Connor agreed. "What was his play about?"

"*Desert Moon over the Desert* was about a moon—seriously—that looks down over the desert—I'm not kidding—and falls in love with a coyote—I'm totally serious. And the coyote falls in love with the moon. Of course the moon and the coyote can never be together, so the coyote howls and howls and eventually befriends a cactus and everything turns out all right."

"Were you in it?" Zion asked.

"Yeah, I played the cactus. My costume was this drab green, so I wasn't bright enough on stage. We had to spray the whole thing down with sparkle spray paint. We had this giant paper moon on the stage with lights behind it, so I was all sparkly and shiny from the light of the moon. It was pretty cool.

"I loved being up on stage, but I had the most ridiculous lines. I still remember them." I recited my lines just as I had done in the play. "Coyote, the moon is many miles away, but I am here on Earth with you. Coyote, my new friend, don't prick yourself on my needles when you give me a friendly hug. Coyote, if you were ever thirsting to death, I would give my life that you may drink my treasured cactus juice."

Zion giggled. "That's awful."

"I'm sure you'll have way better lines in *The Wizard of Oz*," I said.

"Gosh, I hope so."

"No, really. You'll love it. When the play ended and everyone clapped and cheered for us, I felt like I could do anything. I even thought maybe I could have a career as an actress."

"Why couldn't you?" Connor asked.

I gaped at the boys. "How many limbless movie stars do you know?"

Neither one of them said anything. I shook my head and looked at Connor. "By the way, Mom said I could come home with you after school and she'd pick me up before dinner."

"Really?" His face brightened. "I thought you weren't allowed to go to anyone's house where they didn't know the parents."

"My mom said it's okay since she knows you, and your mom works so much and sleeps in the evening. I guess my mom can't really get a good chance to meet her with all that's going on. She is going to be home after school, right?"

Connor shrugged and barked. "Yeah, she'll be home sleeping. She worked a twelve-hour shift last night."

"Has she ever thought about trying to get shifts during the day?" I asked.

"She has to take what she can get right now," Connor said. "And this job pays well." He looked at Zion. "You want to come over, too?"

Zion shook his head. "Dentist appointment." He grimaced.

"The next support group meeting is coming up," I told Connor.

"Support group meeting?" Zion asked.

Connor grinned. "Don't you mean social event, Aven?"

I glared at Connor while I spoke to Zion. "It's just a little group that meets at the hospital every month."

"Sorry, Zion," Connor said. "For freaks only."

"Hey!" I cried. "No one there is a freak. Especially not you."

Connor blinked his eyes, shrugged, and barked. "If you say so, Aven."

I let out a loud breath. "Anyway, my mom's already planning on taking us."

Connor raised his eyebrows. "Such peer pressure. I guess I have to go in that case."

"Yes, you do."

21

CONNOR LET ME INTO THE SMALL
two-bedroom apartment he shared with his mom. I
scanned the room and noted the sparse furnishings—a
three-person couch, a small coffee table, side table,
and lamp. No pictures hung on the walls, and I saw a
couple of unopened boxes stacked in one corner. "How
long have you two been here again?" I asked.

"A little over a year," Connor said. "I know. Mom
works a lot and hasn't had a whole lot of time to decorate or anything. Plus we hope we aren't going to be
here forever."

I tried not to look too sad for Connor when I told
him, "I hope so, too."

Connor barked as we unloaded our bags onto the
small kitchen table. It only had two chairs. Just then,

a bedraggled-looking blonde woman wearing a night-gown and a robe emerged from a small hallway. "You home, baby?" she said. Then she noticed me. She looked both surprised and embarrassed as she pulled her robe closed and tightened the belt. "Oh," she breathed. "You brought a friend home."

"Mom, this is Aven."

She glanced briefly at my torso. "Hi, Aven. I'm sorry I'm not more presentable for you."

"That's okay," I said to try to ease her embarrassment. "Connor told me you had to work all night."

She gazed at Connor. "Yeah . . . I was just coming out to tell him there's a bowl of macaroni and cheese in the fridge for him to heat up for dinner. I'm sorry I don't have more—"

"No, that's okay," I said before she could finish.

"Mom, Aven just came over for a couple of hours to play video games. Her mom will be picking her up before dinner."

Connor's mom looked so embarrassed about the situation that I felt bad Connor hadn't been able to give her some kind of warning about me coming over. "I'm sorry for the surprise, Mrs. Bradley. I'm happy to finally meet you."

"I'm happy to meet you, too, Aven. It's nice to see

Connor with a friend. Perhaps you can come over again on another day when I'm a little bit more myself."

"Oh yeah, I'd love to." I don't know what got into me, but then I said to her, "And maybe you can come to the next Tourette's support meeting with us."

Connor jerked his head at me, and I immediately realized she knew nothing about it—something I think I had already suspected. Her eyes were large with surprise. "Tourette's support meeting?" she said slowly.

Connor shrugged his shoulders. "Yeah, Aven and I went to a support meeting one day while you were working."

"Connor, I wish you would tell me about these things." Her eyebrows furrowed together. "How did you get there?"

"Aven's mom drove us."

"Don't worry," I said, noticing the look of concern on her face. "We're not, like, a psycho family or anything. We're totally normal, except for . . ." I motioned toward my shoulders with my head. "But my parents had nothing to do with that."

She gave me a tired smile. "I'm sure your family is lovely." She turned her attention back to Connor. "I'm happy you're going to a support group, baby. Just . . .

when Aven's mom comes to pick her up, I'd like to meet her, please."

Connor nodded. She went to him and kissed the top of his head. "I'm going back to sleep. Could you wake me up in a little bit so I can make myself more presentable?" Connor nodded again. Then she walked back down the small hallway and disappeared into a dark bedroom.

I turned to Connor. "Your mom's nice. I don't know why—"

He cut me off. "I wish you hadn't told her about the support group. She doesn't have time to go, and now she'll just feel bad about it."

"Why don't you at least give her a chance to decide what she wants to do?"

"She doesn't need any more stress than she already has," he said.

"I don't think the support group would stress her out. I'm sure she's more stressed out not knowing what's going on with you."

"She's better off without having to deal with me."

I suddenly saw things so clearly. It wasn't at all that Connor's mom couldn't stand him, as he had said. It was that Connor couldn't stand himself. He blamed himself for all his mom's problems—his dad leaving, this tiny apartment, her hectic work schedule. I knew he felt it was all his fault. But from what I'd just seen, I strongly doubted she felt the same way. "Connor, she's your mom. She doesn't deal with you. She loves you. Why don't you let her—"

"Why are you always trying to fix me?" Connor snapped. "Why don't you just be my friend, Aven? I don't need to be fixed."

"I don't want to fix you," I said. "I don't think you're broken or anything. I just want to help you. Friends help each other, don't they?"

"I'd rather you just play video games with me. That's how you can help me."

I lowered my eyes and ran my rainbow-striped flat over the dingy carpet. "Okay," I said. "But I won't stop going to the meetings. You can come if you want." I shrugged. "Whatever. I don't care."

Connor's face softened, and he grinned. "Yeah, you do. And yeah, I'll come."

CONNOR AND I WALKED UP TO

the door of the Tourette's support group. "Here we go again," he said under his breath as I opened the door. This month's group was smaller—only Dexter, Jack, and Mason were there.

"Hey, armless Aven," Dexter said.

"Is that a new tic, Dexter?" I asked, thinking of his tendency to say inappropriate things.

"What do you mean?" he said, a baffled expression on his face.

I grinned at the floor. "Never mind."

Dexter patted the seat next to him. "Come sit over here—chicken nipple."

Connor and I sat in two seats next to Dexter. "Where's everyone else?" I asked.

"I don't know," Dexter said. "Maybe Rebecca slapped herself so hard—chicken nipple—that she's lying passed out on her kitchen floor."

Jack snorted loudly. "That's not cool, Dex," he said.

I shook my head. "Definitely not cool."

"I'm sorry," he said, clearly doing his best to look innocent. "It could be the bathroom floor."

"That's enough, Dexter." Andrea looked up from the clipboard she held on her lap. "That's almost crossing the line into making fun *of* instead of making fun *with*." She stared him down, but I could hear some playfulness in her voice.

"I'm sorry." Dexter hung his head and stuck out his lip. "I won't do it again." He covered his mouth to hide his obvious grin.

"Well, it looks like this is all we have today," Andrea said. "Why don't we go ahead and get started. Since we all talked a little bit last month about our fear of going out in public, I thought this month would be a good time to talk about some techniques for staying relaxed when we go out. There's no reason any of you should feel you need to stay confined to your house out of fear of venturing out. It's so important you all live your lives as normally as possible, and feeling comfortable when going out in public is a big part of that."

"But what if we can't relax and our tics get really bad?" Jack said, letting out his loud whooping noise.

"Don't already decide that you can't relax in public, Jack," Andrea said. "That's why I'm going to teach you some techniques you can use. Are you going to tic in public? Probably, yes. You have to accept that. But you don't have to allow it to get out of control."

"Is this going to be about habit-reversal training?" Connor asked. "Because I've already tried that."

"What's that?" I asked him.

Before he could answer me, Andrea said, "No, Connor. We're not going to be discussing habit-reversal training today."

Connor turned to me. "It's when you try to focus your attention on doing something that basically, like, competes with the tic as soon as you feel the urge. Over time, it's supposed to make you feel the urge to tic less."

"Does it work?" I asked.

"A little," Connor said. "But I haven't been very good about doing it."

"It can work well for some kids," Andrea said. "But today we're just going to focus on relaxing."

I ignored her. "Maybe you should try it again if it helped," I told Connor.

"I told you I'm not going to therapy anymore, Aven," he said. "Besides, it didn't work well for me."

I frowned and kicked at my chair legs as Andrea went on about how to breathe deeply. We all closed our eyes, and she told us to breathe in slowly through our noses and out slowly through our mouths. I found it difficult to relax with Dexter repeatedly saying "chicken nipple" next to me, but I did my best.

"Now," Andrea said in a soothing voice, "feel a warmth in your chest—a wonderful warmth that travels from your chest . . . to your shoulders . . . now down your arms . . . and into your fingertips."

I couldn't help it—I totally burst out laughing. Then Connor and the other guys joined me. "You feel that warmth in your fingertips, Aven?" Dexter asked.

Andrea tried to continue talking about the warmth drifting down to our legs and feet, but everyone kept giggling and ticcing, so eventually she gave up and talked to us about other ways we could relax in public. These included using our breathing, visualization, meditation, and even counting or going over times tables.

At some point, Andrea said we should all have a goal we were working toward. It didn't need to be big, but something easily attainable—like my parents had always taught me: one small goal at a time.

Dexter said he wanted to make it through a meeting without calling his mom to check the stove. Andrea said that was a good goal. Then Dexter asked if he could call his mom to check the stove. Jack said he wanted to talk to this girl at school he liked—not ask her out or anything, but just say hi. And Mason wanted to stop making farting noises.

When Andrea asked me what my goal was, Connor and I looked at each other with knowing grins—but I wasn't about to tell the whole group about our murder investigation. Instead, I said I wanted to learn how to use nunchuks, which was also true.

When Andrea asked Connor about his goal, I blurted, "Connor's going to challenge the next person who makes fun of him at school to a cage match."

The others giggled, but Connor squinted at me suspiciously then turned his attention to Andrea. "I guess I should try to get out somewhere," he said. "I haven't been anywhere but school and Stagecoach Pass since I moved."

The way he said his goal felt noncommittal, and I doubted he would follow through with it.

Andrea gave us the last ten minutes to socialize, so everyone wanted me to show them what kinds of things I could do with my feet. Andrea handed me her clipboard, paper, and pen, and I wrote *People with arms are lame*. I also opened up a water bottle and put my hair in a ponytail—impressive stuff.

"Wow, Aven," Dexter said. "You're like a super-hero—like a totally awesome armless superhero."

"If only I had those nunchuks," I said.

"Armless Aven!" Dexter announced. "Able to open water bottles with a single toe!"

I blushed (that darn idiopathic craniofacial erythema). "Not a single toe, but that's okay." I glanced at Connor, but he wasn't smiling. Actually, he looked downright annoyed.

Later, on the way home in the car, I asked him, "What's the matter with you?"

"Nothing." He slumped down in his seat and crossed his arms. "Dexter just thinks he's so funny."

"He is funny," I said.

"I can tell *you* think he's so funny, but I don't." He turned away from me so he could stare out the window. "He's starting to get on my nerves, calling you armless Aven," he mumbled.

"Someone at the support group calls you armless Aven? Is that from his Tourette's?" Mom asked.

"No," Connor said. "It's from his stinky personality."

I looked at Mom in the rearview mirror. I could

tell from her wrinkled, squinty eyes she was grinning. I grinned back and then looked out my own window, hardly able to keep myself from giggling.

I had never, ever in my entire life made a boy jealous until now.

CHRISTMAS AT STAGECOACH PASS was actually pretty cool. My parents decided it was worth it to hire a company to come in and decorate the park with lights and a big tree in the middle of Main Street. We pulled all the old Christmas decorations out of storage and placed them around the park—things like wreaths made of horseshoes and cowboy boots filled with fake poinsettias.

Dad made sure the company he hired strung lights over the covered wagon that marked the entrance. They also added the word **CHRISTMAS** after **STAGECOACH PASS**, so everyone would know something a little different was going on.

I had the idea to set up a booth that sold hot cocoa and s'mores fixings, and we lit fires in a couple of the old metal garbage cans. I had never expected the Arizona nights to get so cold; the weather even dipped below freezing a couple of times. I actually got to wear my ear muffs while I stood outside with Connor roasting marshmallows over the fire—well, he roasted marshmallows for me. I didn't exactly need my toes freezing off.

"It's too bad Zion's gone for winter break," I said. Zion and his family were spending two weeks in New Zealand. They'd gone all the way to the other side of the world to visit the movie sets from *The Lord of the Rings*. My dad had raised an eyebrow when I told him that and said, "I've got to meet these people."

"Zion told me it's actually summer down there right now," I said. "How weird is that?"

Connor didn't answer as he looked around and barked nervously. The roasting sticks he held over the fire shook a little. "This place is busier than ever," he said, and barked. The people roasting marshmallows across from us stared at him.

"Don't let it scare you off," I said.

Connor looked offended. "I won't. I mean, you know, as long as it doesn't get *too* busy."

I raised an eyebrow at him. "What qualifies as *too* busy?"

Connor shrugged. "Busier than this."

"Well, I hope that's not true because I would miss you."

"I'm sure it will be dead again once Christmas is over," Connor said, which was obviously reassuring to him, but not to me. I didn't want the park to get dead again. Connor pulled a marshmallow off the stick and shoved it into my mouth. "Then things can just go back to normal."

"Ah doh wah go nanahol," I said, my mouth stuffed full of marshmallow.

"Huh?"

I swallowed. "I don't want it to go back to normal. I want it to stay busy. You realize if the park closes down, my parents lose their jobs, and we probably have to move again."

Connor frowned. "Yeah, I didn't think of that." He stuffed another marshmallow into my mouth. "Then I hope it stays busy . . . just as long as it doesn't get *too* busy."

We invited Connor and his mom over for Christmas Eve. We held a dinner in the steakhouse and invited all the employees who didn't have any family to spend it with. Mom and Dad ordered three big turkeys.

"What can I do to help?" I asked Josephine, who was ordering everyone around in the kitchen. They were busy making cornbread stuffing, mashed potatoes, corn, and of course, cowboy beans, corn bread and coleslaw (which I would most definitely *not* be eating; coleslaw was ruined for me for life and would forevermore be known as pit slaw).

Josephine handed me a masher. "Why don't you mash up them potatoes?" She stuck the giant pot of potatoes on the floor for me, and I worked on handling the masher with my feet. Several of the employees stopped to watch, but Josephine told them all to skedaddle. "Those will be the best mashed potatoes you ever put in your mouth," she snapped at anyone who raised an eyebrow at me mashing the potatoes.

At one point Henry walked in. He put his hands on his hips. "Aven Cavanaugh!" he scolded. "What are you doing with your feet in the food?"

I didn't think Josephine could have looked more shocked than if a tarantula the size of a horse had trampled through the room. "You crazy old kook!" she said to Henry. "Don't you know her name by now? Get out of here and make yourself useful." She shooed him out of the room, and neither one of them returned.

When I was done with the potatoes, I peeked

my head through the swinging doors of the kitchen. I watched Connor and his mom sitting at a table together with my mom, talking and laughing. I knew this was the first time they had eaten in a restaurant together since Connor's tics had started, so I was glad to see Connor looked so comfortable, although he didn't eat much during dinner.

As we all sat together at the table, I whispered to Connor, "Henry just called me Aven Cavanaugh in the kitchen."

He scrunched up his nose. "Like you said—he gets really confused."

I picked up my fork with my toes and stabbed a big bite of turkey. "I guess. He does keep confusing me for someone else, but why would he think I was a Cavanaugh?"

Connor shrugged. "Maybe you look like a Cavanaugh."

I shoved the bite of turkey in my mouth and chewed as I thought about this. "If only we could find that missing picture from the museum," I said. "Maybe that would tell us something."

"We'll just have to keep searching the storage shed. There's got to be something in all that junk."

I nodded as I stabbed another chunk of turkey. "I hope so."

That evening, Mom and Dad gave me my Christmas present: a pair of turquoise and silver earrings they had purchased from a Navajo woman. I thought if I ever got that necklace cleaned up and maybe got a new chain for it, it would look nice with my new earrings. I also thought this Navajo woman should come and sell her jewelry at Stagecoach Pass. Actually, I couldn't stop thinking of things we should do with the park. I had a lot of ideas.

Later that night, I dragged Dad out to go tarantula hunting. I'd done this several times before; I had become obsessed with finding a live tarantula. He held the flashlight for me so I could sneak up on any holes I had found earlier in the day, thinking they might be tarantula burrows. But I never did find one, no matter how much I searched. I began to wonder if I ever would.

THE FUN AND SUCCESS OF CHRISTMAS

had me thinking a lot about Stagecoach Pass. The park had gotten old and tired. Everyone in town had visited at one point and didn't feel the need to come back. There was no draw—even the food at the steakhouse probably got old because they only served a few different things. Something needed to change or there wouldn't be a Stagecoach Pass for very long. And then who knew where we'd go?

My parents were so busy keeping up with all the little tasks that went into running the place that they didn't have time to see the bigger picture. But I did. As we sat down one chilly January night for dinner together, I told them my ideas.

"You know, I walked through Stagecoach Pass

yesterday, and I counted seventeen empty storefronts," I said as I took a bite of roll. "Seventeen."

Dad sighed. "I know. This place is like a ghost town."

"It makes the place look sad," I said. "We need to get some stuff in here for people to do. Stuff for people to buy."

"It takes money to fill the buildings with employees and merchandise," Mom said.

I frowned. "Can't we take out a loan? I heard you have to spend money to make money."

Dad laughed. "Where'd you hear that?"

"On a commercial."

"Well, that may be true sometimes," Dad said. "But I think the park already took out a couple of loans just to keep going. I'd have to talk to Gary about that, but I don't think it's an option."

"Isn't there some other way to get stuff in here?" I said.

Dad took a swig of his water. "I suppose we could rent the spaces, but then we'd have to worry about finding businesses and what kind of businesses should be allowed to rent here."

"Of course," I said. "We would want it to all be . . . cowboy-ish." I eyed both of them. "You know, I've been writing down ideas for a while now. Ideas for the park."

"We'd love to hear your ideas, sweetie," Mom said.

I went back to my room, grabbed my notebook, and returned to the table. I opened it with my toes. "Things that Stagecoach Pass needs to bring in business," I read aloud. "Number one." I looked at them dramatically. "A lighter food option. We have the steakhouse for a big fat, heavy, greasy meal, and we have the soda shop for a large ice cream sundae when you only ask for a single cone, but there's no deli or sandwich shop or anything like that for a nice little lunch."

I could tell they liked the idea so I went on. "Number two: coffee and smoothies. Whenever Mom and I go shopping, I notice the malls always have some kind of coffee and smoothie place. Number three: more shopping. Navajo jewelry like the earrings you bought me, a cool leather shop, and a hat store that specializes in custom cowboy hats. Stuff like that."

"Wow, Aven," Dad said. "Those are all great ideas. It's just complicated, honey."

"How is it complicated?"

"Well," Mom said, "for one thing, how do we even find these vendors?"

I shrugged and went back to eating my dinner, sorry my ideas had fallen flat. Then I remembered Mr. Jeffries, my art teacher, telling us about an art festival in a town called Fountain Hills that was happening next weekend. He encouraged us all to go and check out the local artists' work. "There's a giant art festival in Fountain Hills next weekend," I said. "There will be like five hundred artists. Maybe we could find some cool vendors there."

Mom and Dad looked at each other. "I suppose it wouldn't hurt to go check it out," Mom said. "Might be fun."

"And what if we had our own art festival?" I said, getting excited now. "With artists and food and music . . . and fireworks!"

Mom and Dad both laughed. "Let's not get ahead of ourselves," Dad said, but I couldn't help it. My mind was going crazy now.

"It's a great opportunity for the artists to check out Stagecoach Pass and see if they might want to rent a space here. Main Street is huge. We could have a huge art festival. You should have it by early April before it gets too hot outside. Oh, and I saw this show about food trucks, and—"

"Slow down, Sheebs," Dad said. "How about we start with visiting this festival and see how it goes from there?"

"But if we're going to have our own art festival, the

best way to let the artists know would be to tell them about it at *this* art festival in Fountain Hills."

"I'd have to get approval before doing anything," Dad said.

"You mean from the dead owner?"

Dad laughed. "Aven! The owner is not dead. And, yes, I'd have to get approval from the very-much-alive owner."

"But I thought you said he gave you total free rein over the park."

"There are also permits and a whole bunch of other stuff to take care of," Dad said.

"Then get on it, Daddy-o. Time's-a-wastin."

He looked at me with pride in his eyes. "My daughter. The ultimate problem-solver."

"You have trained me well, Jedi Master," I said.

"Very good, Jedi . . . learner . . . person."

I rolled my eyes at him. "Not quite, Dad." Zion's parents would have had a way better comeback.

"So, speaking of dead owners," Mom said, "what's going on with your top-secret investigation? Find any more clues about the Cavanaughs?"

"Not really. The guitar was the last thing we found." The boys had brought it up to the apartment for me, and I'd shown it to my parents. They thought it was pretty cool, but it didn't really tell us anything about the Cavanaughs. And just because the last initial was C didn't mean it had belonged to a Cavanaugh. "But you know how I told you Henry always talks to me like he thinks I'm someone else?"

They nodded.

"Well, he called me Aven Cavanaugh on Christmas Eve. Don't you think that's kind of weird?"

Mom and Dad looked at each other. "That is . . . mildly intriguing," said Dad.

"Strange," said Mom. "But he did call me Elizabeth Taylor the other day." She ran a hand through her long, dark hair. "Easy to see how he could make the mistake, of course."

I had no idea who Elizabeth Taylor was, but Dad said, "Absolutely," as he carried his empty plate to the sink. "I have to go check out the old building with the broken-down bull. One of the workers told me they peeked in the window and saw a bunch of mice running around." He groaned. "The keys in the office are all such a mess. I hope I can figure out which one even opens it."

"What keys?" I asked him.

"Keys to the park," he said. "The most important ones are all labeled, but there are about fifty that I have no idea what they're for. I have a feeling I'm going to be there all night trying out keys."

"I didn't know you had all those keys," I said.

"Of course I have keys, Sheebs. I can't run this place without keys."

"Well, it just so happens I'm looking for a key."

IT WAS A RARE ICY COLD WINTER
day as Connor, Zion, and I sat outside the office on the
sidewalk eating our lunches.

"Fruit snack, please," I said, and Connor shoved one
in my mouth. Mom had insisted I wear my old warm
boots today, and though I was glad my toes weren't
freezing, it was highly inconvenient.

I looked at my friends, both shivering as they took
bites of their lunches. "This is ridiculous," I said. "We
should be eating in the cafeteria today." They looked up
at me in alarm. I had to admit I didn't feel ready to head
there myself despite the freezing wind. "We can stay here."

They both let out sighs of relief.

"So Dad told me he's going to try to get the keys in
the office as organized as possible, and then he'll let us

try out the ones he can't figure out. I bet one of them goes to the desk."

"I wonder what's going to be in there," said Zion.

I chewed on a fruit snack and gulped. "Maybe a murder weapon."

Zion shivered. "I hope not."

"I hope *so!*" I declared. "Then we can turn it into the police and then they'll get the fingerprints off it and then they'll bust the murderer and then we'll all be in the newspaper. And the murderer will be like, 'I could have gotten away with it, too, if it hadn't been for you nosy kids!'"

Zion and Connor both frowned at me. "I don't want to be in the newspaper," said Zion.

"Me neither," said Connor. "And I think you've watched too much *Scooby-Doo.*"

I scowled—sometimes those guys were a total buzzkill. And I *had* watched too much *Scooby-Doo.* I decided to change the subject. "So, we've had hundreds of artists call about the festival. So many that we've had to turn some away that don't fit with the Stagecoach Pass theme. Seriously, like who wants to buy something called a diaper cake? Uh, no, thank you. I'll stick with chocolate."

Zion nodded. "Yeah, that's gross."

"Disgusting," Connor agreed.

"We need to find a band now," I said. "Any ideas?"

"Shouldn't be too hard to find one," Connor said. "Just look online." Then he raised an eyebrow at me. "Maybe you should perform, Aven."

I looked at him in disbelief. "Is that supposed to be a joke?" My ear muffs slipped down a little and Connor pushed them back up on my head.

"No," he said. "I think it would be cool."

Zion looked at me. "What do you play, Aven?"

"The guitar," Connor answered for me. "But she won't play for anyone. I think she might be lying about being able to play."

I shoved Connor with my foot. "Shut up."

He laughed. "Then play a song at the festival. It would be so cool."

"What do you care?" I said. "You're not even coming."

Zion's head jerked to Connor. "You're not going?"

Connor shrugged. "I don't know. Aven thinks there's going to be, like, thousands of people there."

Zion stared at him. "So?"

Connor gaped at Zion. "So? So, that's thousands of people to stand around staring and laughing at me."

"They'll be staring at me, too," I said. "But I'm still going."

"Fine," Connor said. "I tell you what—if you play your guitar, I'll come and watch you."

My throat suddenly felt dry. "Juice box, please," I whispered, and Connor obliged. I took a swig and cleared my throat. "I'm not performing at the festival. I would never perform in public for anything."

"Then I'm not coming," Connor said stubbornly.

Darn it. He knew I wouldn't perform and that was his way out.

"Why won't you play for anyone, Aven?" Zion said.

I shrugged. "I don't want people watching me up there." *Watching the freak*, is what I wanted to say.

"Why not?" Zion asked. "You acted in a play on stage in front of people."

"That was different. I was in a silly cactus costume. If you didn't know me, you wouldn't have even known I didn't have arms. Doing stuff with my feet in front of a crowd, performing with my feet . . . that's just different. I'd feel like I was in a circus or something."

"That's silly," Zion said. "No one would think of you like that."

But I knew he was wrong.

IN MOST PLACES, SPRING COMES

around March or April or even May. Arizona's whole winter is pretty much like springtime with a few winter days scattered throughout. I can't say I was sorry not to have to trudge through snow everywhere I went.

Things were really coming together for the festival. Dad found a website that had like a hundred country western bands for hire listed on it. We had our pick, and they weren't even very expensive. Mom and I spent an entire day cleaning up the old stage in the closed down rodeo arena. That was also where the food trucks would park, since we weren't having a rodeo.

Connor and I had gone to two more support group meetings, and I got the feeling he was actually starting to enjoy them, even though he often gave Dexter the stink eye.

I still hadn't found a tarantula despite going out almost every night with Dad. One day I was visiting Spaghetti, and I asked Denise what she knew about tarantulas. "Do they bother the animals?"

"There aren't any tarantulas around here," she told me as she raked the dirt ground.

"There aren't? But I thought they were all over the desert. I've read all about them, and every book I've read distinctly states that they live in the Sonoran Desert."

"They *should* be here, but I guess with the city moving in on us like this, they've gone away."

I rubbed at Spaghetti's sides with my feet. "Yeah, but there's still a good chunk of desert right behind us. I'm always looking for one when I walk out there, but I've never seen one."

Denise stopped raking and wiped her brow. "I guess there used to be a bunch around here, but they disappeared a while back. Henry says it was around 2004."

I stared at her. "They disappeared in 2004? But Henry can't remember anything."

"Nothing recent," Denise agreed. "But sometimes he can remember things from the past."

"In 2004," I repeated to myself.

"Yeah," he said 'The last time anyone saw a live tarantula around here was in 2004.'" Denise went back to raking the ground. "Who knows? Probably just made it up."

I decided to go visit Henry. He was sitting in front of the soda shop in one of the rocking chairs. I stood in front of him and asked, "When did the tarantulas disappear?"

"In 2004," he said quickly and matter of factly.

"Why do you think that?"

"Because," he said, and for the first time ever, his eyes looked clear and knowing to me. "They left with her."

I shivered, and not from the cool breeze. "With who?"

He looked up at me, his eyes once more clouding with confusion. "Who what?"

"Who did the tarantulas leave with?"

He continued giving me his confused look. "You want an ice cream, sweetheart?"

I sighed. "No, thank you."

I even visited Madame Myrtle to try to figure things out, but she was clueless about the tarantulas. She said maybe an exterminator came and took care of them in 2004. Ridiculous.

Connor, Zion, and I spent as much time in the

storage building as we could, looking through old pictures and junk. So far, Dad had given us about fifteen unlabeled keys to try out on the desk, but none of them had worked.

"This one's a dud," Connor called, pulling a key out of the drawer and tossing it back into a paper bag.

I frowned as I kicked a box in one corner of the shed. It was so old and brittle from the heat that it burst wide open, sending a wave of papers onto the floor. It wasn't necessarily the most orderly way of doing things, but it was a lot easier than Zion's methods. I sheepishly glanced over at him as he carefully removed old tape from a box and pulled the top back like the *Mona Lisa* might be inside.

Zion shook his head at me. "Aven," he scolded, "do you have to make this place look like a tornado ripped through here?"

"She's from Kansas," Connor said as he tried another key. "Tornadoes are in her blood." Connor grunted and then barked. "Dud." He pulled the key out.

I sifted through the papers on the ground with my toes, trying to make out the faded writing. There were a lot of numbers and words like *deduction* and *revenue* and *net*. I had no idea what any of it meant, but I decided it was all far too boring to be important.

"Whoa," Zion said, causing Connor and me to stop what we were doing and look at him. He had a book in his hands and was pulling something out from between the pages. "Whoa," he said again in a whisper.

Connor and I walked through the junk to see what Zion was *whoaing* about. He held up an old black-and-white photograph for us to see.

A photograph of me.

With arms.

Wearing the turquoise necklace.

Taken in 1973.

27

I SHOWED MOM THE PICTURE THAT
evening. She stared at it a long time before whispering,
"It could just be a coincidence." She didn't look like she
believed her own words.

She sat down at our little kitchen table without
taking her eyes off the picture. "She has your face, but
it's in black and white. Maybe her hair is a different
color."

"Don't you think it's strange, though?" I said.

She nodded. Then she set the picture down. "It
must be a coincidence. I saw this show once about
doppelgangers—"

"What's that?" I asked. Sounded dangerous and
exciting.

"Just people who look alike."

Oh, not that exciting.

"Anyway," she went on, "there are people who look alike all over the world. Like, literally identical. But when they were DNA-tested, they found out they weren't related at all. Just totally random."

"That's weird," I said. "I guess I found my goppledinger."

She smiled. "Doppelganger."

I thought for a moment. "I wonder if Henry knew this girl and that's why he keeps thinking I'm someone else."

She looked from me to the picture and was about to say something when Dad walked in. "Mean Bob has officially left the building," he announced. "And good riddance."

"What a relief," Mom said. She got up and handed Dad the picture. "Aven found this in that storage room."

Dad stared at the picture a long time before looking at me. "Odd," he said. "You found this in that desk?"

"No, none of those keys worked. We found it stuck in a book in a box."

He didn't say anything more, but I did notice the way he and Mom looked at each other. And their faces weren't very happy.

ZION'S MOM DROPPED HIM OFF at Stagecoach Pass early Saturday morning, and then Mom took us to pick Connor up at his apartment. He was already outside his door when I walked up the concrete path.

"Hi," I said, meeting him in front of the apartment as he turned to lock the door.

He struggled with the old lock. "Hey." He followed me out to the car and peeked his head in the front window. "Hi, Mrs. Green," he said before getting into the backseat with Zion.

"Hi, Connor," Mom said and pulled away from the curb. "Are you excited for our little adventure? I know I am—anything to get away from Stagecoach Pass right now and all the craziness of this festival planning. I seriously need a break from that place."

Connor gave me a hesitant glance. "Aven and Zion won't tell me where we're going."

"Well, then," Mom said, "I don't want to ruin the surprise."

Connor seemed relaxed as we drove through Scottsdale. We spent most of the drive talking about Arizona and how we liked it here.

"I'd never seen a saguaro cactus until I moved here," I told them, thinking of the great saguaro at the top of my hill. "Well, one that wasn't me anyway."

That got us talking about *Down and Dirty in Kansas City* and the total lameness of *Desert Moon Over the Desert* again.

It took us a long time to get to the movie theater. As we pulled up in front of it, Connor no longer looked relaxed. I knew he was angry. "Aven, I told you I don't ever want to go to the movies," he said, his eyes blinking rapidly, shoulders shrugging.

"Connor, just wait—" I said.

"I'm not going in!" he nearly shouted at me.

Zion slumped down in his seat and stared at his lap.

"Calm down, Connor," Mom said gently. "We have

a special surprise for you. You don't have to worry about upsetting any other movie watchers."

Connor huffed. "Of course I do. I can't go to the movies."

"Yes, you can," Mom said. "Don't you trust us?"

Connor glowered at me, his ticcing increasing by the moment. "Yes, but—"

"But nothing," Mom said. "Let's go in. We're seeing that new sci-fi movie you guys want to see so badly."

Connor threw his head back against the seat rest and ticced and huffed some more while Mom parked the car. We got out and walked up to the ticket booth, where Mom quietly spoke with the cashier for a minute before buying four tickets to the movie. Connor barked a lot as we walked through the lobby. It was early, though, so only a few bystanders were around to gawk at him. People didn't seem to notice me at all when Connor was around. I felt bad for Connor, but I also enjoyed the feeling of being invisible.

As we entered the theater, Mom said, "It appears you have your pick of seats." The theater was completely empty.

Connor looked at me and Zion. I smiled at him. "Mom had to call a lot of theaters until she found one that was willing to let us have the whole theater to ourselves."

"Are you serious?" said Connor.

"Well," said Mom, "we couldn't afford to rent out the whole theater, so it was a lot to ask. But the manager here has a son with Tourette's and was really understanding. Plus, he said the morning show was usually fairly empty, so we were able to work it out."

I could see the darkness lift off Connor like a blanket as his eyes lit up. And that alone made everything so worth it. "For real?" he said. "We have the whole theater to ourselves?"

"For real, Connor," said Mom.

Connor put an arm around Mom's shoulders. "Mrs. Green, you're the coolest!"

"I know," she said casually. "Now you three go and find a seat. I'm going to sit way in the back where I like it."

"Can we go get some popcorn?" Connor asked, and I knew he must have been incredibly happy to ask for food.

"Heck, yeah," I said. "I want some popcorn. And some gummy bears."

"Gross," said Zion. "You like those?"

"Heck, yeah," I said again as we walked out of the theater. "I love squishy gummy candies. I love Hot

Tamales, too. My dad says I like them because they're red like my hair and hot like my temper." I laughed.

Connor grinned. "That's great to know. We'll try to stay on your good side."

"Who says you're on it?" I narrowed my eyes at the two of them.

"I was just hoping we were." Connor shrugged his shoulders and blinked, but it made me happy to see that, despite being out in public, his tics weren't completely out of control. I hoped that meant he was starting to feel a little more comfortable.

"I bet your parents want to see this movie, Zion," I said.

"Are you kidding? They went to the midnight showing on opening night. They waited in line for like four hours, too." He rolled his eyes. "*And* they wore costumes."

Because it was so early, we didn't have to wait in line to get our snacks. Mom had given me some money that morning, and I told Zion to reach his hand inside my purse and get it out. I also let the boys handle the transaction. It was kind of nice not having Mom there, making me do everything.

Zion paid for our popcorn, sodas, and gummy bears. Twenty dollars poorer, we headed back to the theater, Connor's and Zion's arms stuffed full of treats. Mine . . . not so much. I stopped at the bathroom on the way back so I could wash my feet since I knew I'd be dipping them in the popcorn.

As we sat waiting for the movie to start, the three of us surreptitiously glanced back at Mom sitting in the very back row. "Do you think she might be hiding something from you?" Connor said in a hushed voice. "And why did she cover herself in napkins?"

I giggled. "It's warm enough outside to wear short sleeves, so she forgets to bring a sweater when we go places, and it's so cold inside from the AC. She calls the napkins her blankets." I rolled my eyes. It was even more embarrassing than when my great-grandma in Kansas used a flashlight to get around in the movie theater. "She does it at restaurants, too. At least here no one can see her."

"Do you think she has any idea at all who that girl might be and she's just not telling you?" Connor asked.

I looked back at her, all covered in her "blankets," a goofy smile on her face. "No. I don't. She seemed totally surprised. My parents would tell me if they had any idea what was going on. She said it's probably just a coincidence." I told them about doppelgangers.

"I still don't buy it," Connor said. "What are the

odds that you would end up here at this park and find your doppelganger?"

"Well," I said, "I found this article online about these two guys who ended up sitting next to each other on a plane. They looked identical. And then there's that one movie star who everyone thinks is a vampire because there's a picture of a man who looks just like him from World War I."

We lost interest in Mom and plopped back down in our seats. "I know what happened!" Connor suddenly declared, making Zion jump in his seat. "There's a portal up on the hill. You go through the portal while you're wearing that necklace you found and go back in time to 1973. While you're there, you have your picture taken." Connor looked extremely proud of himself as he barked and said, "That's it. I've totally solved it. You could run into your grown-up self at any time, so you better be careful."

"Why do I need to be careful?" I asked him. "Is my grown-up self dangerous?"

"*Clearly*," Connor said. He looked at Zion for confirmation.

Zion nodded. "Yeah. I'm pretty scared of grown-up Aven. Why wouldn't she just come and tell us all of this if she's wandering around somewhere? I mean, you'd remember us, wouldn't you?" Zion asked me, like what we were talking about was actually true.

"Maybe she's dead," Connor said.

I smiled at him. "Rodeo clown mafia?"

"Totally." We giggled.

I stuck a piece of popcorn in my mouth with my foot and chewed. "I really love this whole theory. Especially since this magical portal makes me grow arms."

Connor's face fell. "Oh, yeah. I didn't think of that."

"You never know what a magical portal might do," Zion said, and Connor's smile returned.

I decided to take advantage of Connor's good mood. "So are you coming to the festival or what?" I asked him.

"I already told you."

"I know, I know," I said. "Just thought I'd double-check."

"Well, you can stop double-checking," Connor said, "because the only way I'd go into a crowd like that would be if someone, like, tied me up and dragged me there."

Zion grinned at Connor. "Don't give her any ideas."

Zion seemed to know me pretty well already.

I OPENED THE FRONT DOOR TO let Connor in. He trudged into the apartment, his shoulders slumped. He looked so depressed, I thought he might burst into tears.

"Is everything okay?" I asked him.

He shrugged, and I couldn't tell if it was a tic or if he was deliberately being evasive. He leaned against the wall, not looking at me and let out a bark.

"My parents are taking a big piece of fence out of the rodeo arena so the food trucks can get through. I've been working on that stupid report for language arts."

He just stared at the kitchen floor.

"Hey, guess the name of the band we got to play for the festival," I said, hoping he'd snap out of whatever funk he was in.

He shrugged again.

"The Flap-Jackeroos." I laughed. "They normally do gigs for, like, Waffle Houses and stuff, but I guess the country western breakfast entertainment business isn't booming, so we got them to do the festival. Cheap, too."

He still didn't look at me.

"Is everything okay with your mom?" I asked.

He finally spoke. "Yeah."

"Did something happen at school?"

He didn't answer me—just barely shook his head. Hoping I could cheer him up, I said, "Hey, I have a surprise for you."

He followed me into the living room. I sat on the edge of the small couch, my guitar at my feet. "Sit down." I motioned with my head for him to sit beside me. He dropped his backpack on the floor and flopped down on the couch with a big dramatic sigh.

I plucked at the strings with my toes for a second and adjusted one of them. I took a deep breath, willed my pounding heart to slow down, and began to play. I had practiced "Moon River" every day for the last month, but I still managed to hit a wrong note here and there. It sounded okay, though, and Connor was completely quiet as I played.

Completely quiet.

When I finished, I looked at him. "You didn't tic the whole time I was playing," I said almost in a whisper—like if I spoke any louder, it would shatter the fragile quiet, and Connor would unload all of the tics he had bottled up while I played.

I had thought he would be so happy I had finally played for him after all the times he had asked me, but I saw he had tears in his eyes. "Maybe you could bring the guitar to school and follow me around playing music everywhere I go." A single tear escaped and ran down his cheek. "Then I could stop being a freak."

In my whole life, I had seldom felt like I was missing out on anything by not having arms. Some of the only times I had ever wished for them were during those fleeting moments of frustration when my shirt got caught around my neck or some insensitive person tossed something at me without thinking, only to have it bounce off my chest or head.

But at this moment, as I watched the tear slide down Connor's cheek, I felt the true loss of not having arms. Because I couldn't reach over and wipe it away. And I wasn't about to do it with my foot.

"What's wrong?" I asked.

Connor shook his head. "I could never do anything like that," he whispered.

"Sure you can. You can play the guitar. I'll teach you."

"No," he wiped at his cheek, "that's not what I meant. Aven . . . you don't understand. It's like it doesn't even matter that you don't have arms. You still play the guitar and go to museums and restaurants and do all kinds of stuff. I can't do anything. I can't even go out in public."

"Of course you can. Look at all you've done lately— going to the meetings and the movies and coming here all the time. You can even come to the festival. You can do anything."

"No, I can't!" Connor snapped, jumping up from the couch. "I won't ever be able to do anything with my life. I won't ever be an actor or a politician or a teacher or anything like that. Geez, I can't even go to the movies without renting out the whole theater!"

My mouth hung open in disbelief. "Why would you want to be a politician?" My great-grandma would have been appalled. I could just see her raising her wrinkled fist in the air and warning Connor about the coming revolution.

Connor gazed back at me, so much sadness in his eyes. "You want to know why I was so upset when I got here?"

I nodded. "Yes."

His ticcing was getting bad again. He shrugged his

shoulders manically as he spoke. "I walked . . . to the store before coming here. I wanted to get you some gummy bears."

I gaped at him. "You stopped at the store by yourself? For me? To get me gummy bears?" I know it sounds silly, but to me this was like the equivalent of him going to Antarctica and back to bring me a feather from a penguin's butt.

He struggled to get the words out now. "I saw . . . someone . . . filming me . . . on their . . . phone."

My stomach dropped like it did when I rode a roller coaster. "What?"

"Yeah . . . Aven . . . they were filming . . . the freak."

I shook my head slowly, not wanting to believe it. "Maybe they were doing something else."

"They weren't!" he yelled. "So you see . . . I can't do those things. Because . . . I'm a freak. Next week I'll be . . . on YouTube with a bunch of snarky comments about . . . what a psycho I am. I'm never going out in public again! Not to school! Not to the meetings! And I'm not going to your stupid festival!"

"Stop it." I tried to stay calm. "You're not a freak. No more than I'm a freak. You can do anything you want. Go ahead and become a politician if that's what you want. What's stopping you?"

"This!" he cried as his ticcing continued unabated.

I shook my head. "No. You're just upset because of some jerk with a cell phone. You can do anything, Connor."

"And you're unrealistic to say I can do anything I want. I know your parents . . . have led you to believe you can do whatever you want, but it's not true. You can't be a basketball player or a surgeon . . . or an astronaut."

I glared at him. "Why couldn't I be an astronaut? Because I'm a girl?"

"Because you have no arms, Aven!" he shouted at me in exasperation like he was revealing some shocking secret I didn't already know.

I gritted my teeth. "Don't tell me what I can or cannot do, Connor."

"Oh, really?"

"What's that supposed to mean?"

"How come you won't play your guitar at the festival? How come you won't eat in the cafeteria?"

"I choose not to play the guitar or eat in front of people. It's not because I can't."

"I don't believe you."

I glared at him. "We're supposed to encourage each other, Connor. That's what friends do. I'm sorry some disgusting person was filming you at the store, but you have no right to tell me what I can't do because—"

"Because of your disability," he finished for me. "Because you're disabled, Aven. Like me."

I stood up to face him. I don't know why I let what Connor said infuriate me so badly. I had been called disabled before. People had referred to my disability a hundred times. But it was like he had used the word to insult me. I could feel my bad temper rising and taking control. "I swear if I had arms right now I'd punch you right in the face!" I cried. "I'm not disabled! I'm . . . abled!"

"Why are you so mad?" Connor said. "I'm just stating a fact. I'm disabled. You're disabled. Everyone at that stupid support group is disabled. I'm just telling it like it is."

"Well, go tell it somewhere else and don't come back!" I yelled at him.

"Fine." Connor could barely get the word out because his ticcing was so bad at this point. He grabbed his backpack, took out the bag of gummy bears, threw it on the floor at my feet, and flew out of the apartment.

And I suddenly felt incredibly sorry.

I TOTALLY AVOIDED CONNOR THE

next day at school. Actually, I didn't have to avoid him because I didn't see or hear him anywhere. I wondered if he had meant it when he said he was never going to school again.

So it was just another day with everyone staring at me but no one talking to me. Another day of eating lunch in the stupid bathroom. I didn't even want to see Zion and have to explain anything. I couldn't wait for school to end—I nearly ran to the bus when it was over.

As soon as I got home, I sat down at my desk. I browsed through several of my most recent blog posts. No comments from Emily. No comments from Kayla. No comments from any of my old friends. My old world had moved on without me.

I typed my next post.

I know I totally make light of not having arms. I mean, what good does it do to complain about it all the time? This is my life. I can't change it. No arm transplant can be done. I am who I am and it's all I've known and all I'll ever know. No big deal.

I'm sure you're thinking, *Yeah, but come on, not having arms must really suck at times.* Yeah, not having arms does suck at times. A lot of what stinks about not having arms are little things— things most people take for granted because they have arms. So here it is—the twenty worst things about not having arms:

1.   No smacking people no matter how badly I may want to. I don't think stomping their toes provides quite the same satisfaction.

2.   No boxing matches. If I had arms, I think I would have been a professional boxer.

3.   Doing my hair is difficult. I would love to try

some styles I can't do—like a cool fishtail or a dramatic updo. I read the term *dramatic updo* in a magazine once.

4. Everything takes longer.

5. No basketball.

6. No shaking hands with people when I meet them. I would make sure I always had a firm handshake. Then again, I don't have to worry about sweaty palms.

7. Using large tools like chainsaws and weed whackers is likely out for me. I know the instructions say not to operate if you're under the influence of drugs or alcohol, but they should probably say not to operate if you're under the influence of drugs or alcohol or don't have arms.

8. Strappy tank tops and dresses don't look quite right. And mannequin arms don't help either.

9. Reaching things on the top shelf.

10. My back hurts because it's hard to exercise your back muscles without arms.

11. My feet get sore. I think I have arthritis already. Feet aren't meant to be used the way I use them day after day all day long. Unless you're an ape.

12. Nonhandicapped people using the handicapped stalls in the bathroom. I need the extra room, and it sucks to wait until their perfectly armed selves are all done with their luxurious, roomy bathroom visits.

13. No pushing a heavy wheelbarrow. I'm sure one day I'll be mad about this, though it hasn't happened yet.

14. Splinters are a real pain in the butt.

15. No hand or arm massages. I hear they feel super good.

16. Harder to keep my balance.

17. Harder to do . . . everything.

18. No wiping away a friend's tears when he's hurt.

19. No hugging him to make him feel better.

20. No reaching out for him when he walks out the door.

THE SKY WAS ALREADY TURNING

pink as I lay on my bed. My chest felt like my giant saguaro was sitting on it. I heard the front door open and shut, and then a second later Mom burst into my room. "I have the greatest idea," she blurted out before she saw my face. "Oh, honey, what's wrong?" She rushed to the bed and sat next to me.

I frowned. "Nothing."

"Nothing's been wrong for two days. Now tell me what nothing is," she demanded.

My eyes filled with tears. "When Connor was here yesterday . . . he called me disabled."

Mom scrunched her eyebrows. "Well . . . okay. Did that make you angry?"

"Yes."

"Why?"

"Because," I said, trying to hold back more tears. "I know I am. I don't need other people telling me I am and telling me what I can or can't do."

"I'm sure he didn't say it to hurt you."

"I don't ever want to be seen just as a disabled person," I said. "I don't want to just be Aven Green, that girl with no arms. I don't want to be labeled like that."

"I think Connor would be the last person to label you like that. You shouldn't get so offended if someone calls you disabled, Aven. You *do* have extra challenges that others don't have. It *does* take you longer to do most tasks. Your movements *are* limited. There's a big difference between saying you're disabled and saying you're incapable."

"Well, he tried to say I was incapable of becoming an astronaut."

She laughed and stood up off the bed and faced me. "I think it would be extra challenging for you, but I don't think it's impossible, not with robotic arms and all that." She did a robot dance to show off what I assumed were some ridiculous robot arms that would never be of any use to any astronaut. "I don't think anything's impossible for you," she said as she continued her display.

I smiled and then remembered I was angry. "If you're trying to make me laugh, it won't work." My scowl deepened. "Connor thinks everything's impossible for him, and he's all mad about it, so he tried to act like everything's impossible for me, too. He's being a big baby and feeling sorry for himself."

"Shouldn't you try to be a little more understanding, then? You're his friend, Aven. You should be building him up when he gets down on himself."

"He wasn't building me up," I said. "He was trying to tear me down."

"I don't think he wanted to tear you down at all. Like you said, he did it because he was feeling bad about himself. I'm sure he feels terrible about the whole situation now. Stop being such a hothead."

"Look who's talking," I muttered.

"Watch it, little lady," Mom said sternly as she reached over and rubbed her knuckles over my head.

"Ouch." I huffed and pushed her hand away with my foot. "What was this big idea you had, anyway?"

She looked excited again as she remembered what she had burst in here to tell me in the first place. "I spoke with the Flap-Jackeroos. I told them all about you and how you love to play the guitar, and we thought it would be wonderful if you joined them for a song." She threw her hands over her mouth and let out a little squeak like she had just said the most exciting thing of all time.

I scowled. Seriously, this again? "I don't think so, Mom."

Her face fell, and I felt bad for a moment about disappointing her. "Why not?"

"I'm not going to go up on stage so people can come gawk at the girl with no arms playing the guitar. I'm not some circus show."

Mom's face was instantly furious. "Aven!" She looked appalled at what I said, and I immediately felt guilty for having said it. "How can you say that? I wanted you to join them for a song because of how proud I am to have you for my daughter, because I want everyone to see how amazing you are, not because I want to make a spectacle of you. What's the matter with you?"

"Everything," I said. "Everything is the matter with me." I got off the bed and stormed out of the apartment.

I walked around Main Street as the sky turned dark, ignoring the few visitors who still ambled around. I didn't want to go home. I kicked the dirt and huffed and sulked as I wandered aimlessly. I sulked about my fight with Connor. I sulked about hating school. I sulked about missing my old school and friends. But mostly I sulked because Connor was right—I was disabled and no one would ever see me as anything else. I would never be able to do all the things everyone else could do. I would never be able to be a surgeon or an astronaut or an actress, no matter how angrily I proclaimed I would be.

I stopped when I saw Spaghetti and pressed my head to his. "You're the only one who understands me," I whispered.

I continued walking around until I got to an old wagon that sat in a quiet corner of the park. I climbed into it and sat down. I stayed there all through dinner until Dad walked up and got into the wagon with me.

"Mom's worried about you," he said. "She saved you a plate of spaghetti."

I *humphed* as dramatically as I could. "I'm not in the mood for spaghetti."

"Me neither," he agreed. "You know she didn't even remove his fur. Gross. Do I have a llama hair in my tooth?" Dad pushed his lips up and leaned in about an inch from my face to show me his teeth.

"Ha-ha," I said. "I happen to know he's right over there in the petting zoo and was not the main entrée at dinner. So go tell your bad jokes somewhere else."

He sat next to me quietly for a long time, and I could almost hear his mind working, trying to come up with something to talk about. Finally, he said, "I heard soccer tryouts are day after tomorrow."

"Oh, you *heard* soccer tryouts are day after tomorrow?"

"Yes, I heard after I called the school several times and put the date on my calendar a few weeks ago and called again today to make sure it was still correct and then put a reminder in my phone."

"I'm not trying out for soccer, Dad."

"Oh, I don't think you should try out. No way. I just thought I'd mention it so you would know to avoid the tryouts. I wouldn't want you to accidentally stumble into a soccer tryout and accidentally make it onto the team or something like that." He tapped the side of the wagon. "That would be awful."

I frowned as hard as I could beside him. I wasn't going to let him destroy my terrible mood.

"It sure is a beautiful night," he said. "Look at all those stars."

I looked up. "What stars?" I snorted. "You can't see any stars in this stupid city."

"Look right over there." He pointed at the sky. "I see one right there."

I rolled my eyes. "I think that's a planet, Dad."

"Oh, yeah. I think you're right. Jupiter?"

"I think so." I turned my head to another light in the sky. "That might be Venus."

Dad looked at me. "What's wrong, Sheebs?"

I sighed and bit my lip. "I just . . . I feel so messed up right now. I wish my life were simple like everyone else's. Do you think . . ." I bit down harder on my lip, trying to keep it from quivering.

"Do I think what, honey?"

"Do you think it would have taken two years for someone to adopt me if I had arms?"

"I think it would have taken about two seconds for someone to adopt you if we'd have found you sooner, arms or no arms. You were our daughter and you were waiting for us. That's all there is to it."

"I just wish I were like everyone else."

He stared at me for a while. "Now that's a terrible thought."

I scowled. "How is that terrible? Connor wants to be like everyone else." I tried my best to keep the tears from spilling out by not blinking. "And so do I."

Dad put his arm around me. "Why do you want to be like everyone else?"

Despite my best efforts, a tear broke loose and slid

down my cheek. "So I can wear cute tank tops and play the guitar at the festival and not worry about everyone staring at me all the time." I took a deep breath. "So I don't have to eat in the bathroom ever again."

Dad furrowed his eyebrows. "And why do you have to eat in the bathroom, Aven?"

I wiped at my cheek with my shoulder. "Because I don't want the other kids to see me."

Dad sighed deeply and looked back up at the sky. "Those lights up there . . . they're not like anything else in the sky." He looked at me. "But they shine the brightest."

I sniffled. "That's so cheesy, Dad."

He laughed. "It may sound cheesy, but it's true." He squeezed me tightly to him and made a ridiculous wise look, rubbing his chin thoughtfully. "No one lights a lamp and hides it under a basket. They put it on a table so it can shine for all to see."

I rolled my eyes. I'm sure it pleased him to no end to incorporate a Sunday school lesson into our discussion. "Okay, Dad. I'll go sit on a table."

He kissed the top of my head. "Don't be like everyone else, Aven. Be you."

"And what is that exactly? A table lamp?"

"No, not a table lamp." He poked me in the ribs,

causing me to squirm beside him. "A light who shines for all to see." He tilted my chin to look up at him. "A light who doesn't hide in the bathroom."

He got down from the wagon. "Come home when you're ready. Just know Mom will be pacing the floor until you get there."

I smiled a little and hunched down in the wagon until I was sure he couldn't see me over the rim. I heard him chuckle and walk away. I looked at the wall of the wagon next to me and noticed someone had scratched something into it.

I eased my foot slowly out of my flat and ran my shaking toes over the engraved words. Inside of what looked like a heart, someone had written *Aven was here.*

I thought back to that first box Connor and I had found in the storage room and the letters on it: A, V, N. Connor had been right all along.

Aven. Not Cavanaugh.

I SAT WITH ZION OUT ON THE
sidewalk at lunchtime the next day.

"Do you know where Connor's been?" he asked,
popping a potato chip into his mouth. He offered me
one and I took it from him with my toes. "I haven't
seen him the last couple of days."

I stared down at my lunch, slowly chewing the
potato chip. "I don't know."

"What's wrong?" Zion asked.

"Why would anything be wrong?"

"How come you don't know where he is?"

"It's not like I know where he is at all times." I
snorted. "I'm not his all-the-time-watcher . . . person."

Zion raised an eyebrow at me. "Aven," he said in a
scolding tone.

I sighed. "Okay, fine. We got in a fight."

"What about?"

I shrugged. "He hurt my feelings. I hurt his feelings. So everyone's feelings got hurt. That's all." I looked up at him. "It was a misunderstanding."

"You better fix it," Zion said.

"I can't fix anything if I can't find him."

"He's got to come back to school at some point."

"And when he does . . ." I trailed off. What would happen then?

"And when he does?" Zion prompted.

"And when he does, I'll make it right."

I walked into the Saloon and Steakhouse after school and sat at the bar. The bartender, fully bedecked in cowboy gear (even though I knew he was just a regular old college student), raised an eyebrow at me. "Give me a stiff one, Charlie," I said.

I could tell he was holding back a smile. "Aven, you know you can't sit at the bar."

I groaned and dropped my head forward onto the old wooden bar. My forehead hit the shiny, polished oak with a loud thump. "It's a stupid rule," I muttered, pressing my forehead to the cold wood.

"It's not my rule," Charlie said. "It's the . . . what's

that thing called? Oh, yeah, the law. It's the law." He pointed at a nearby table. "Go sit over there and I'll bring you your drink."

I got down from the barstool, dragging my forehead off the bar as I went. "You better put extra cherries in it today," I said, flopping down at the table.

A minute later, Charlie placed my drink in front of me. "One sarsaparilla for the forlorn redhead. Extra maraschino cherries."

I frowned. "What makes you think I'm forlorn?"

He touched my forehead. "You've got a big fat red spot on your face from bashing it on the bar." He walked back behind the counter to tend to a couple of customers.

I sadly swigged down my sarsaparilla through the straw Charlie had kindly provided. When the drink was nearly gone, I made deliberate slurping sounds as I tried to get the last of it up. The people at the bar stared at me, but I didn't care; I slurped louder. I think I was trying to drown out the sounds of the annoying player piano, which I wanted to kick to death at the moment.

"Now that is the most theatrical display of melodramatics I have ever seen in my life."

I looked up and found Josephine standing in front

of me. I sat back from my empty drink. "Sorry," I mumbled.

Josephine pulled out a chair and sat down across from me. "You want to tell me what's the matter?"

I shrugged. "Why would you think something's the matter?" I asked, frowning so hard it hurt the muscles in my face.

"Oh, I don't know. Could be you've been moping around this place for the last few days like someone died."

"No one died." I stared at the red-and-white, plastic checkerboard tablecloth. "My friend is mad at me."

"Oh," she said. "The one who barks all the time?"

I nodded.

"You two seem to be pretty good pals. I'm sure ya'll will work it out."

I raised my eyes and looked at Josephine. I realized I knew absolutely nothing about her except that she had worked at Stagecoach Pass since it opened. Despite seeing her all the time, she was always too busy to ever speak to me. I didn't want to lose this chance to get any information I could. "Do you have a family, Josephine?" I asked her.

She looked surprised at the question. "Uh, no. No, I don't."

"Have you ever been married?"

She smiled. "Never had time for that nonsense."

I nodded in agreement. "I don't think I ever will either."

She laughed. "Only thirteen and already knows she won't ever marry." She slapped the table. "It figures."

"What figures?"

Josephine looked like I had just caught her letting out a gigantic fart or something. "Oh, nothing. Just young people these days."

I stared at her. "You've worked here a long time, haven't you?"

"Yep. Just about sixty years."

"Wow," I said. "That's so long."

"Yes, it is.

"And you've always worked in the restaurant?"

"Oh, no. I've done all kinds of jobs around here. Just about everything there is to do."

"Were you ever the fortune-teller?" I asked.

She laughed. "Well, maybe not *everything* there is to do."

"Why do you stay here?"

She drummed her fingers on the plastic tablecloth. "I guess I like it here."

I studied her face. "So you were here in 1973 then?"

She stopped drumming her fingers and tilted her head a little. "Sure. Why?"

"Do you remember a girl who was here? A girl who looked just like me but with arms? I know this sounds crazy, but I think her name was Aven, too."

This seemed to make Josephine uncomfortable. She shifted in her seat. "I don't . . . I don't really recall." She pushed away from the table and stood up.

"You know who I'm talking about, don't you?"

"I really got to get back to work," she told me. "Those cowboy beans won't serve themselves."

"Wait!"

But she was already gone.

THE NEXT DAY AFTER SCHOOL, I

made my way to the bus, hoping I would find Connor on it. Instead, I found Dad standing in front of it, waiting for me.

"What are you doing here, Dad?" I asked him.

"I brought you this." He lifted a bag he had strapped over his shoulder and hung it around my neck. "It's got your shorts and T-shirt in it, shin guards, and Mom ordered you brand new cleats with Velcro."

I sighed. "Dad, I—"

"I'm not saying you have to go try out," he said. "I'm just giving you the option. You can either turn around and make your way to the field over there or you can carry this bag onto the bus and go home." He kissed my forehead. "It's your choice, Sheebs." I watched him walk away.

I stood there on the sidewalk as the kids poured into the buses, my soccer bag hanging around my neck, still hoping I might see Connor.

I had loved soccer from that very first kick in second grade. I was so good at it, it almost felt like I was cheating because I use my feet for my hands and you're not allowed to use your hands in soccer. But don't tell anyone.

Soccer ended up being the good bonding experience Dad had always wanted for us. He would practice with me at home after school, and we would watch soccer games on TV together (after *The Lone Ranger*, of course). We had fun cheering on Brazil. I don't know why we cheered on Brazil, but I think it was because they call it football instead of soccer. Dad said that made so much more sense. I asked him what football would be called, then, if soccer was called football. "Man smash," he said.

Dad and I weren't the only ones who loved it, though. Mom always came to all my games. She was like one of those embarrassing crazy people you hear about who take kids' sports way too seriously. She would constantly yell at my coach and my coach would threaten to ban her from the games. The coach was my dad.

"You getting on or what, Aven?" the bus driver asked, startling me.

It was hard to think about putting myself out there again, trying to be a part of a new team, at a new school, with a new coach. Everyone watching me. But there are a lot of hard things in life. Who would I be if I gave up when things got hard?

I'll tell you who I'd be—the Queen of Sheba.

I looked up at the bus driver. "Not today," I told him and turned and walked away.

34

I DROPPED MY BAG ONTO THE BENCH by the field and walked over to a cluster of soccer balls. I pulled one out of the group with my foot and started dribbling it around slowly. I glanced at a small group of girls who were also trying out for the team. They were all talking and laughing together.

I went back to dribbling the ball around, focusing all my attention on it, trying not to think about the group of girls standing on the other side of the field.

"Hi," I heard someone say from behind me. I stopped the ball with my foot and turned around—it was the girl I had briefly spoken with in science class on my first day of school. She had her long brown hair pulled up in a ponytail. "Aven, right?" she said.

I breathed heavily from working with the ball. "That's right."

"I'm Jessica," she said, tightening her pony tail. "We were watching you with the ball."

My stomach sank. Of course they were watching me. I tried not to let my shoulders slump. "Oh?"

"You're really good. How long have you been playing?"

"Oh," I said, a little more brightly. "Since about second grade. How about you?"

"This is my second year. I'm sure you'll make the team."

I hoped my smile wasn't so big that I looked spastic. "You think so?"

"Definitely. You have really good control over the ball."

"Thanks."

"You're going to love being on the soccer team," Jessica went on, like I had already made it. "It's so fun when we have away games. Last year we did makeovers on the bus, and we prank-called Coach Fuller on her cell phone from the back. That's her over there." Jessica pointed at a short, stout, gray-haired woman, who was intensely studying a piece of paper on the other side of the field. "After like the tenth time we did it, she started yelling, 'I'm going to call the cops on you, you hoodlum!' Everyone on the bus could hear her." She laughed. "It was hilarious. Olivia filmed her on her phone." She gestured at the group of girls. I assumed one of them was Olivia. "We'll show you the video. It's so funny."

"That sounds like fun," I said. "I hope I make it."

"You'll love it. We also have pizza parties, and last year we had a team slumber party."

Coach Fuller called us over to get started.

"I guess we'd better go," I said to Jessica.

She smiled at me. "Yeah, let's go." She motioned for me to follow her, and even though I walked beside her on the way to the coach, I felt more like dancing.

DAD DROVE ME HOME AFTER

soccer tryouts. He had shown up when they ended like he'd never had any doubt I would go try out.

What a know-it-all.

He beamed and asked a million questions as I described every detail of the tryouts to him in the car. When we got to Stagecoach Pass, he opened the center console and pulled out an envelope. "I found this in a drawer in the steakhouse," he said. He turned the envelope over, and I saw that one word was written on it: desk.

"They don't fit the desk in the office." He opened the flap on my book bag and slipped the envelope inside. "Let me know what you find in there, Sheebs."

I ran as fast as I could to the storage shed, before I lost the last bit of light creeping in through the filmy windows. I slipped a foot out of my flat and opened my book bag. I removed the envelope and slid my toes inside. I pulled out a ring with two small keys hanging off it. I felt like I was playing one of those impossible carnival games as I attempted to slip one of the keys, held between my toes, into the hole in the desk.

It finally fit and I pushed it all the way in with the bottom of my foot. It took all my strength to turn it, and it hurt the skin on my toes. But the key turned in the lock. I pulled the bottom drawer out and looked inside—another stack of papers. I pulled those out, barely able to read any of them in the failing light. But underneath the stack, lying on the bottom of the drawer, was a framed picture. I carefully lifted it out with my feet and laid it on the floor in front of me.

It was of two red-haired women. They stood in front of the steakhouse, and they had their arms around each other. The older one I clearly recognized, the other I didn't. But I could see my face in hers. She wore the necklace. And she was pregnant.

I slipped the picture into my book bag and carried it home. Mom was already putting dinner on the table when she turned and gave me a huge smile. "So? How did it go?"

For a moment I didn't know what she was talking about. "Oh, soccer?"

"Of course, soccer." She laughed. Then her face fell. "Did it not go well?"

"No, it went great."

"What's wrong?" she asked.

"I opened the desk," I told her. She stared at me silently. "I found a picture in there. It's in my bag."

Mom immediately lifted my bag off me and carried it to the table. She opened it and pulled the picture out. She studied it intensely.

"I know where it goes," I told her.

We walked to the museum together, and Mom pressed the picture against the empty space in the wall: *The Cavanaughs, 2004.*

The year I was born.

Mom let out a big sigh. "After you showed Dad and me the picture of that girl, we worried maybe it was something like this. But we weren't sure. And we didn't know who would have . . . We even tried contacting the adoption agency we used, but your old birth certificate and any identifying records were sealed. They couldn't tell us anything. We hadn't decided what else to do about it, yet."

"I don't know what to do about it either," I said. "Do you think she knows?"

Mom turned to me and ran a hand down my hair. "How could she not?" She put her hands on my shoulders and squeezed. "Do you want to go talk to her?"

I looked at the older lady in the picture. I needed to know. And my parents needed to know. I took a deep breath. "Okay," I whispered.

"Do you want me to go with you?"

I looked up at her. "I think maybe I should go alone."

Mom nodded. "I understand."

I made my way to the steakhouse, the photo in my bag. I watched as Josephine took an order from a table and then followed her back to the kitchen.

She noticed me as she placed a couple of burgers on her tray. "Whatchya doin' back here, Aven?"

"I need to talk to you."

"I'm awfully busy." She pushed through the swinging doors back to the dining room. I followed her out to her table.

I waited while she placed the burgers in front of her customers. "I need to talk to you," I told her again as I followed her back into the kitchen. I could have easily walked away, but I wouldn't let her, or my nerves, scare me off.

She stopped and folded her arms. "Now what could be so important that you would interrupt dinner like this?"

I stared at her, my heart racing. "I won't leave until you talk to me."

She made a big frustrated sigh and led me to the restaurant's little office. "Better make it quick," she said. "I've got tables out there waiting."

I placed my bag on the desk, opened the flap, and pulled out the framed picture with my foot. It was heavy. My toes trembled, and it started to slip. Josephine reached out and grabbed it before it could drop. She slowly turned the picture over in her shaking hands.

"I *know* you know her," I said. "Please tell me the truth."

"Yes." Her eyes filled with tears as she stared down at the photograph. "I do."

"This was taken the year I was born. And I found another picture. When she was my age. She looked just like me. She's my mother, isn't she?"

Josephine nodded.

"And you're both Cavanaughs," I said.

She nodded again. "Yes," she whispered. "She was my daughter."

"That means . . . you're my grandmother."

She looked up at me from the picture. "I am."

"Is that why I'm here now? Are you the one who brought us here?"

"You're here because I just wanted to see you. To meet you."

I shook my head. "What for? Were you ever going to tell me?"

"No."

I took a deep breath and let it out slowly. "I'm so confused. So where is she anyway? Is she somewhere around here?"

"She's gone," Josephine said. "Died a few weeks after you were born."

"Oh," I breathed. I had always assumed my parents had given me up because of my disability. I had never considered that my mother had died.

"I told her it was too soon to do a show, but she wouldn't listen to anyone. No one ever told her she couldn't do something." She wiped at her eyes. "No, sir," she added in a whisper. "We think she had a dizzy spell because it was so unlike her to fall off a horse like that."

I bit my lip. "I'm sorry."

Josephine shook her head and waved a hand in the air.

"What about my father?" I asked.

Josephine shrugged. "Don't know. Aven never told me who it was. You see, she always wanted a baby but never did find anyone she wanted to marry. She was getting older, and I guess she decided to take things into her own hands. She said I did it all on my own and she could, too. She was always like that— take charge, do everything on her own, no one tell her otherwise. She's the one who named you Aven." Josephine laughed. "She said men do it all the time. Why shouldn't her daughter be Aven, too? She was a firecracker.

"When she died, I didn't know what to do. I was gettin' on in years already and had this park to look after. I didn't think I could provide the attention and care a baby like you needed. So I thought it would be best to let a nice family adopt you."

"So you just let me go," I said.

"Yes."

"Into the foster care system for two years."

Her eyes filled with tears. "I didn't think that would happen. All I thought was that a nice, loving family would want to adopt a baby like you."

"A baby like me," I repeated.

She shook her head. "Oh, I'm saying everything all wrong."

I sighed. "It doesn't matter now. You were right— a nice, loving family did adopt me, and that's all that matters. So how'd you find us anyway?"

"Well, I never could stop thinking about you, wondering how you was doing." She looked down at the desk, her cheeks turning pink. "So I, uh, hired someone to find you some years back." She looked up at me like she was checking on my reaction and then looked away again. "He's been, uh, giving me regular reports about what's been going on with you."

"So you've been stalking us?" I cried.

"No, no, no, no, no. Not stalking. Just checking to make sure y'all was okay. That's how I found out your daddy had been out of work for a while and y'all was about to lose your house."

"We were?" I asked, surprised at the information.

"Of course they didn't tell you. They're good parents."

"Yes," I said. "Yes, they are."

"So I got this plan forming in my head to ask your daddy to apply for this job. I hadn't been managing the park for years. I just couldn't do it after . . ." She looked down at the picture. "Anyway, I prefer to be in the restaurant just working, keeping an eye on things. Sort of secret-like. My old park manager didn't have anything under his hat but hair, so I was relieved to see your daddy had worked as a restaurant manager. I thought it was worth a shot. I didn't know if he'd apply. I'm glad he did."

"How come he doesn't know you're the owner?"

"Oh, I go by Joe Cavanaugh for all my business dealings, but around here I'm Josephine Oakley. Gives me an air of mystery, don't you think?"

I stared at her, not exactly sure what to think.

"If they all knew who I was, they'd be bothering me about every little thing like they used to. I just couldn't handle that anymore. Only my accountant, Gary, knows the truth. I prefer it that way." She ran a hand through her dyed red hair. "And Henry, but his mind's goin'. No one else around here worked back when Aven was here, and I thought I did a good job of making sure no one would ever know who I was." She smiled at me. "I should've known you'd figure it out, smart as you are. Just like her."

I took a deep breath. "So what now? Do you expect me to call you grandma or something?"

"Oh, heaven's no. I never even planned on telling

you who I was. I'm leaving Stagecoach Pass. It's time for me to retire. Over eighty years old and still working like a dog. Stick a fork in me; I'm done."

"Where will you go?"

"The Golden Sunset Retirement Community about five miles from here." She nodded. "Yeah, they have a swimmin' pool and mediocre cafeteria food. I guess it'll do." She stared at me. "I don't expect you to want me in your life. I'm just glad to know y'all are doing okay now."

"What are you going to do with Stagecoach Pass?" I asked, worried my parents would be left without jobs again.

"Well, it's yours."

I stood up straight. "What do you mean?"

"I mean you own it. Right now it's under your parents' control, but when you turn eighteen, it's all yours to do with as you please."

"Are you serious?"

She nodded. "You're my only family. It's all I can do for you."

"This land is worth a lot of money." I stuck my chin out. "Maybe I should just sell it and leave."

"You can do that if it's what you want."

I was quiet for a moment. "No. No, I don't think I will. I kind of like it here."

"Aven liked it here, too. You know she used to play the guitar and sing? She used to do shows here for people."

"I play the guitar, too."

She smiled. "I'm not surprised."

"So, Aven—she was a performer?"

"Oh, yeah. She didn't just sing with her guitar. She rode horses in the rodeos. She loved being the center of attention."

"Tell me something else about her."

Josephine grinned. "She loved tarantulas."

IT WAS A LOVELY, PERFECT EVENING

as I kicked the row of soccer balls into the net one by one. I really was starting to like Arizona—the constant sunshine, the smell of orange blossoms in the air, the soft green grass I walked on barefoot whenever I could. And the beautiful sunsets. I gazed up at the evening sky after I kicked the last ball into the net. It looked like it had been painted with watercolors of pink, orange, and purple. I sighed.

"Nice work, Green," Coach Fuller called. I ran over to Jessica, and we worked on moving the ball back and forth between us as the other girls took their turns at the net.

"We're going to have a team kick-off party at my house this weekend," Jessica said breathlessly as we worked. "Wanna come?"

"Yeah," I said. "Should I bring anything?"

"Mmmm . . ." Jessica paused with her foot on the ball. "How about some soda?"

"Okay. And do you think you might come to the festival?"

"Oh, yeah. I'm pretty sure most of the team is planning on it."

"Good job today, girls," Coach Fuller said.

I checked the watch around my ankle. "Wow. That flew by. I guess I'll see you tomorrow."

Jessica looked past me and didn't answer. I turned around when I heard a bark and spotted Connor standing at the edge of the field. "Is he your friend?" she asked.

Connor raised his hand in a wave, and I smiled. "Yeah," I said. "He's my best friend."

She kicked the ball to me as she grinned and raised her eyebrows. "He's cute," she said and ran off to join the other girls headed to the locker room.

I let out a breathy laugh and walked over to Connor. I stopped about three feet from him. "Hi."

"Hi." He looked down at his feet then back up at me. "You made the soccer team."

"Yeah, I did."

"And you made a new friend." He gestured toward Jessica, still walking back to the locker room with everyone else.

I glanced at her then turned my attention back to Connor. "Yeah." I studied the painful look on his face. "But I miss my old friend."

Connor smiled and shrugged his shoulders.

"Where have you been?" I asked.

"Just home. I decided I was never coming back to school."

"What made you change your mind?"

"You," he said. "And my mom. She told me to get my butt out of bed yesterday. I thought she was going to drive me to school, but instead she called into work and we spent the day together."

"You did?"

Connor nodded. "Yeah, we even went out for dinner."

"Seriously? At a real restaurant?"

"Yeah. Well, sort of. We got take-out and ate it in a park. But still."

"But still," I said. "It's a good start." We stood there awkwardly for a moment. "Guess what?"

"What?"

"Josephine, the lady who works in the steakhouse—she's my grandmother."

His mouth hung open. "What?"

I nodded. "Yeah. She's Joe Cavanaugh. She's the one who hired my parents."

"Why?"

"She said she wanted to meet me and make sure I was okay."

"So who was the girl in the picture?"

"My birth mother."

"What happened to her?"

"She died," I said, surprised to feel the knot in my throat. Surprised at how much I wished I could have known her.

"I'm sorry, Aven."

"Josephine gave me up because she didn't think she could care for me. I guess she thought she was doing the best thing for me."

"I'm sure that's what she thought at the time," Connor said. "But obviously she regretted it to have brought you out here."

"Well, if she thinks she can just have a relationship with me after all this time, she's mistaken." I dug my cleat into the ground.

"Of course," Connor agreed. "She must be a terrible person."

"Well, uh, um, I don't . . ." Connor grinned at me, and I narrowed my eyes at him. "I see what you're trying to do here. I don't think I'm ready to forgive her for abandoning me."

"She didn't exactly leave you in a cave in the desert. How old is she?"

"Eighty-three."

"So she was seventy when you were born. I bet she was thinking, 'Holy cow pie. I'm gonna be near ninety by the time this here baby graduates high school. She'll hafta push me in my wheelchair to the ceremony. That's gonna be hard to do with her feet.'"

"Your Texas accent is awful."

"You get my point," he said.

"Maybe I do; maybe I don't." I smiled at the ground, kicking at the dirt with my cleat. "Everything is really coming together for the festival. I think it's going to be a big success."

"Anything you do would be a big success, Aven."

My cheeks flushed at the compliment. "I'm just sorry you're not going to be there." I looked up at him. "It won't be the same without you."

"I'll think about it, okay?" he said. "That's the best I can do."

"I guess I'll have to accept it then."

We stood there quietly for a minute. "My mom's going with me to the next meeting," Connor said.

"That's so great."

"Do you want to come with us?" He frowned. "I'm sure Dexter would love for you to be there."

"I'd love to be there for you. Not for Dexter."

"Are you sure? Because I know he's *so* funny and all that."

"I'm sure," I said. "And he's really not that funny."

Connor smiled. "I was also thinking maybe you could teach me a little bit on the guitar. See how it goes."

"I'd love to."

"My mom and I watched this video online about people with Tourette's and how music can be almost like a therapy for them. It can even make them stop ticcing while they're doing it. When I told her about you and the guitar, she thought it would be a great idea for us to work together on it. She really likes you."

"That's amazing," I said. "I mean, about the music, but also your mom. She's getting involved."

"Yeah. Because I'm letting her. You were right."

"It's because I'm so smart." I tossed my hair back over my shoulders.

"Yes, you are," Connor said. "Even smart enough to be an astronaut."

THE MORNING OF THE FESTIVAL,

I woke up before it was light out. I had so much to do, and I couldn't wait to get started. The first thing I did was sit down at my computer and write a blog post.

Come to Stagecoach Pass today for our festival! We'll have good food and art and fireworks! It will be the most fun you've had since the last super-fun time you had!

I was frustrated for the first time in a long time at how long it took me to get my jeans on. In my excitement, I kept missing the button with my hook, but I eventually got it and rushed out of the apartment and downstairs.

Mom and Dad were already up and out in the park, making sure everything was in order. When Mom saw me, she said, "Get back upstairs and eat some breakfast."

"I did," I said.

"Liar," she said back.

I made my way to the petting zoo to visit Spaghetti. I petted him with my foot and whispered to him, "It's going to be a busy day." He lifted his head and looked at me lazily then laid it back down like he was saying, *Maybe for you.*

I walked around Stagecoach Pass all morning, trying to be useful, running errands for anyone and everyone, delivering messages, and making phone calls.

By nine o'clock, I was light-headed with hunger, so I sat down with Josephine in the kitchen of the steakhouse and ate a bowl of beans. "Today's your big day," she said.

I scooped a spoonful of beans carefully into my mouth, holding the spoon with my toes. "I forgot to ask you about something," I said.

"What's that?"

"I found an old necklace up on the hill. It's silver with a turquoise stone in it."

"Was that still up there? We released Aven's ashes at the top of that hill. That was her favorite necklace, so I hung it on a little wooden cross. I figured it would be long gone by now—probably washed away in a monsoon. Could I see that necklace sometime?"

"Sure." I put down my spoon and pushed the bowl away from me. "I'd better get going." I left the kitchen, hoping the awkward feeling I got around Josephine would go away in time.

I walked outside and was disappointed to find people weren't already pouring in at the entrance—and more disappointed that Connor wasn't out there. Around ten o'clock, a few people trickled in. As the morning wore on, the trickle became a steady flow.

The Flap-Jackeroos started playing on the newly cleaned stage around noon. I had no idea what to expect of breakfast entertainers, but they weren't bad. And except for a song about bacon or eggs benedict thrown in here and there, they mostly played normal country music.

By late afternoon, the parking lot was fuller than it had ever been. I wandered around, enjoying the festivities and talking to the vendors about their art.

I found Zion, and we ate an obscene amount of junk food together in the rodeo arena. He was normally so strict about what he ate, so I was glad to see him relax a bit about that.

We watched the large group of kids in the petting zoo. Some of them even gave Spaghetti a little attention, though he didn't seem to care much.

I introduced Zion to Josephine and Henry, shot a rubber snake at the shooting range, and even stuck my face through a wooden painting of a cactus so Zion could take a picture.

And everywhere we went, I looked for Connor.

At six o'clock, I left Zion and made my way into the apartment to get changed for the evening events. Mom and I had gone shopping together the day before to pick out a new dress for the festival, and she had laid it out on my bed for me, perhaps worried I might pick something else to wear at the last minute.

With a thumping heart, I carefully slipped the dress over my head and shimmied it down, tugging at the bottom with my toes. It took me a few minutes to get it all straightened and smoothed out. I stood up and looked at myself in the mirror over my dresser.

Mom walked up from behind and put her arms around me. "I like this look on you," she said. "But it's missing something." She pulled a necklace out of her pocket and placed it around my neck—it was the turquoise necklace. I could see she had had it cleaned and had replaced the chain. "It looks beautiful with your pink dress."

"Thanks, Mom. That was sweet of you to do this for me. You know, this was Aven's favorite necklace."

"Was it? Well then, it's extra special, isn't it?" She squeezed my shoulder.

I gazed at myself in the mirror, wondering if I was really going to go out in front of other people looking like this.

"You know," Mom said. "I heard there are a lot of people out there who came today because of your blog."

I looked up at her. "*My* blog?"

"Yep. They said they love it."

"I don't know why. I don't have anything very interesting to say."

Mom cupped my cheeks in her hands. "You, Aven Green, are the most interesting person I know." She kissed me on the nose.

As I walked toward the door, she said, "Would you like a sweater, Aven? It might get a little chilly tonight."

I shook my head. "My shoulders have been covered long enough. They need to breathe."

She walked to me, slipped a finger under one of my spaghetti straps and snapped it. "Yes, they do."

The sky looked like cotton candy as I made my way downstairs. I loved all the sounds and smells of the festival—corn dogs and kettle corn and chili and funnel cakes. Walking over to the Flap-Jackeroos, I ran into Jessica and a large group of girls from soccer.

"You guys came," I said, smiling hugely.

"This is great, Aven," Jessica said. "And you look amazing."

"Thanks." I blushed at the compliment. "You should come watch the music."

As they walked behind me, I spotted Zion sitting at a table by himself, munching on a box of popcorn. I walked with the girls over to him and introduced them. He mumbled a hello to the girls as he stared at his feet and tried to hide his popcorn behind his back.

I made my way to the stage and stood at the bottom of the steps. When the lead singer of the Flap-Jackeroos saw me, he told the audience they had a special accompaniment, and I walked up the stairs to join them. He placed my guitar in front of a chair on the stage for me, and I sat down.

But it wasn't my guitar. It was the guitar we had found in the storage room hidden under the old desk. It was the guitar that had belonged to my mother. It had been cleaned, repaired, and restrung. I looked out into the audience and saw my parents watching me. Mom put her fingers to her mouth and blew me a kiss. I slipped my feet out of my flowery flats and carefully plucked at a string with one not quite steady toe.

We played "Tumbling Tumbleweeds," which I had been feverishly practicing all week, even though my part was quite simple. A large audience formed to watch as we played, and I saw that all their eyes were on me—me in my strappy pink dress. Me in my mother's necklace, playing my mother's guitar. Me with terribly flushed cheeks, beaming as the lead singer winked at me while we played. I looked out into the crowd and saw Jessica and the other girls watching me with excited faces. I saw Zion smiling and waving and I nodded back. I saw my parents, arms around each other, swaying to the music.

I saw Josephine watching me from the very back of the crowd. She had a painful look on her face, and I wondered if she was thinking about her daughter. I tried to imagine how hard it would be for a woman who had been in her position, having just lost her only daughter, already "gettin' on in years," as she had put it. I thought about what Connor had said. She probably truly believed she was doing the best thing for me.

So I decided maybe I would visit her at the Golden Sunset Retirement Home when she left. Maybe we could share a meal of mediocre cafeteria food. Maybe swim in a pool full of old people. I smiled at her, and the painful look on her face seemed to dissolve.

And then, right in the center of the crowd, slowly making his way to the front, I saw Connor. He wasn't ticcing, even though he was completely surrounded by people. He looked totally at peace while I played.

When the song ended, and the audience clapped for us, I stood and took a bow. The lead singer pointed at me and clapped, causing the audience to clap louder. And so I bowed again.

I ran off the stage and straight into Connor at the bottom of the stairs. I felt exuberant and full of energy I couldn't contain. "Come on!" I said to him. "The fireworks are starting soon." We ran away from the stage and found Zion toward the back of the crowd. He joined us as we ran past the gold mine (overseen by a new man named Ramiro who did *not* hate children), where lots of little kids were aggressively focused on finding real Stagecoach Pass gold. We took the trail out to the desert and the three of us made our way up my mighty hill, lit at this point only by the light of the full, shining moon.

We were almost at the top when I saw something out of the corner of my eye. I stopped and stared at the ground just in time to see what looked like a monstrous spider scurry into a hole.

Connor turned around. "What?"

My heart beat rapidly—from the performance, from running up the hill, from whatever it was I might have just seen. "I thought I saw something."

"Tell us about it later," Connor said. "We need to hurry."

When we got to the top of the hill, I sat down beside my saguaro, and Connor sat beside me, and Zion sat beside him. "I knew you'd come," I said to Connor.

He laughed. "I didn't even know I would until about an hour ago." He looked at me in the moonlight, blinking his eyes. "But I'm really glad I did." He let out a bark.

"Me, too," Zion and I both said at the same time.

Connor looked down at the city lights. "You spend a lot of time up here, don't you?"

"Yeah. Yeah, I do. I come up here when I need to think or be alone. Up here I can see things clearly."

"What do you see?" Connor asked.

I looked down at Stagecoach Pass then back at Connor and Zion. "I see two of the best friends I've ever had."

Zion smiled, his white teeth gleaming in the moonlight.

"So I'm glad we came here," I said. "And I'm glad for everything that's happened. Because if it hadn't, I wouldn't know either of you. And I'm glad I know you."

Connor's hazel eyes flashed from the very first firework. "I'm glad I know you, too, Aven."

"Me, too," Zion said.

As the fireworks exploded over the lights of the city—millions of lights for millions of people—I didn't feel so insignificant anymore. I felt as big as the giant saguaro beside me. I felt like I was shining, and this time I thought maybe it wasn't just the moon. Maybe the light was in me.

I SAT AT MY DESK, STARING AT MY
computer screen. "When I'm done with you, there
won't be anything left to snore," I heard the cowboy
outside shout. I smiled, remembering my prank with
Connor. It seemed like so long ago.

As the gunshots fired off outside, I gently tapped
my toes on the keys and hummed "Tumbling Tumbleweeds" to myself, thinking about what I should write.

Thanks so much to everyone who visited
Stagecoach Pass for our festival yesterday. It was a
wonderful day and one I know I won't ever forget.

Over the last several weeks, I've been getting
more and more emails from other kids like

me—kids without arms. A lot of them are looking for advice about all kinds of things, but I'd say most of the emails are about school—everything from making friends to handling homework assignments to dealing with mean comments and the "looks."

I've thought about it a lot, and I came up with a list of twenty supplies you need to survive middle school when you don't have arms. So here it is:

1. Good shoes. Ease of removal is of utmost importance here. Ease of reapplication—equally important.

2. Sense of humor. I'm being very serious here— you've got to have one. Seriously.

3. A sizeable daily breakfast. You never know when you might chicken out in the lunchroom. Get your daily fuel requirement early in the day.

4. Easy-to-eat bagged lunches. Do you really want to carry that giant tray through the cafeteria?

And forget about bringing stuff like chili and clam chowder for lunch. Really. Forget. That.

5.   An easy-to-carry/open/close/get-things-out-of book bag.

6.   Lots of cute shirts. This really applies to both people with and without arms. And when you're ready—tank tops.

7.   Bully spray. Similar to bear spray, only better. Would be great to have for those nasty little comments. I'm totally inventing this.

8.   Thick skin. More like armor. Armor skin.

9.   An e-reader is super helpful. And no more toe paper cuts.

10. Some kind of sport or recreational activity— soccer, dance, swimming, professional hopscotch. You can do it! I'm trying out my motivational speaking skills here.

11. Pants that button easily. Trust me, when nature calls at school, you'll be grateful you listened.

12. Your handy-dandy hook. From buttoning pants to lifting a dollar out of your pocket, a good hook is essential.

13. A wide variety of nail polishes. Boys probably don't care much about this, but when people are staring at our feet as much as they do, we want to look our best. Am I right, ladies, or am I right?

14. Nunchuks. At least until bully spray becomes available.

15. An open heart and eyes. You think you're the only one out there who feels different? What about that kid sitting alone in the library or out on the sidewalk?

16. Awesome parents. This is a must.

17. Friends who listen.

18. Friends who laugh with you.

19. Friends who are brave.

20. Friends who love you just the way you are.

These last few supplies are hard to find, but when you do find them (and I sincerely hope you do), hold on to them forever. Don't ever let go.

I felt a hand on my shoulder and looked up to find Mom standing behind me. "I didn't know you were there, you sneak," I said.

"I like your latest post."

"Thanks. Oh, and I finally thought of a good name for my blog. *Aven's Random Thoughts* is kind of lame."

"So what will this world famous blog be called then?" she asked.

"*The Unarmed Middle Schooler's Guide to Survival.*"

She laughed. "I love it. And I can guarantee there's not another blog out there like it."

"Nope," I agreed. "I'm totally an original."

CONNOR, ZION, AND I WALKED
down the crowded sidewalk at school. It was lunchtime, and everyone milled about, carrying lunch bags. They congregated in the grass, eating their sandwiches.

We discussed our plans for the weekend. The guys were going to help me come up with a memorial for Aven to put at the top of the hill. I thought it would be a nice surprise for Josephine. I was also going to start teaching them how to play the guitar. Connor hoped it would help his tics, and Zion hoped it would help him with the ladies.

"We already have five shops rented out from the festival," I told them. "Really great artists, too."

"That's awesome," Zion said.

"And I've been thinking about how dead Stage-coach Pass is over the summer," I said. "It's just too hot for people to come and walk around, so I've been at the outdoor malls taking notes about what they have to offer that still draws people in during the summer, and get this." I jumped in front of them. They both stopped and gave me their full attention. I waited a moment for tension. Finally I said, "Splash pad," with serious dramatic flair.

"You want to put in a splash pad at Stagecoach Pass?" Connor said.

"Not a regular splash pad," I explained. "Like an old-fashioned splash pad."

"Oh, yeah," Zion said. "Like the splash pads they used to have that Billy the Kid brought his kids to."

"Ha-ha," I said. "I mean instead of a regular splash pad, it would have, like, a water-pumping windmill and a little creek that runs around it and maybe even a fort with a water slide or something like that. It would, of course, have to stick with the Stagecoach Pass theme."

"That's a great idea," Connor said.

"Yeah. And we could plant some big trees around it with picnic benches underneath for the parents to sit. And then if we get our sandwich shop and our smoothie place, they'll have something to pick up for lunch. I also thought we need a store that sells old-fashioned toys. Like really cool ones. It could be quite the summer outing for families."

"You know, Aven," said Zion, "I think one day you might be running that place."

"Are you kidding me?" said Connor. "She already is."

"Oh, and another thing," I said. "I'm going to learn how to ride a horse."

"Cool," said Connor.

"Awesome," said Zion.

And you know what? They didn't look surprised at all.

Jessica walked by us. "Hey, Aven," she called, and a couple of girls walking with her waved at me.

"Hey," I said. "See you guys at practice later."

I saw that we were walking by the cafeteria. I stopped. The guys stopped and both gave me questioning looks. I looked at Connor. I looked at Zion. And I walked to the doors. "You guys want to eat lunch together?" I said.

The corner of Connor's mouth tipped up a little and he barked. He walked to the doors and opened one for me. "Ladies first?" he said, almost as if he were asking me if I had thought this through—if I was certain.

I smiled at Connor, stepped forward into the door-way, and entered a cafeteria I had never seen before. After all, there was a lot I needed to do with my life. I had places to see, things to try, new friends to meet.

And light to shine.

ACKNOWLEDGMENTS

Thank you to my supportive agent, Shannon Hassan, for picking Aven out of the slush and falling in love with her. To my brilliant editor, Christina Pulles, whose insight and direction made this book so much better. To Ryan Thomann for designing a beautiful cover. And to everyone at Sterling who worked so hard for this book: Hannah Reich, Ardi Alspach, Sari Lampert Murray, Maha Khalil, Chris Vaccari, and the entire sales team. Thank you from the bottom of my heart.

Thank you to my friends and family who read early versions of the book. To two inspiring ladies: Barbie Thomas and Letisha Shelton. To my husband for always supporting me. To my children for filling my life with humor. To Kyle, always. And most of all, thank you to God, from whom all good things come.

Lastly, thank you to my awesome readers. I hope you enjoyed reading *Insignificant Events in the Life of a Cactus* as much as I enjoyed writing it!

1 Think about the title of the book. Why is it called this? What does Aven mean when she says her life is an insignificant event in the life of a cactus?

2 How do you think your life would be different if you didn't have arms? What kind of obstacles would you have if you didn't have arms? How would you overcome them?

3 This book is told in the first person, from Aven's point of view. How do you think it would change if it were told in the third person? Do you notice any differences between the way Aven talks to the reader and the way she writes her blog posts?

4 If you had a blog like Aven's, what would you write about?

5 When Aven first meets Connor, and he points out that she doesn't have arms, she says, "Oh my gosh! I knew I was forgetting something today."

Can you find other examples in the story where Aven makes light of not having arms? Why do you think she does this?

 When Aven starts her new school, a girl asks her if her disability is contagious. Why does she ask this? If you were Aven, how would this make you feel?

 Why does Zion eat alone on the sidewalk behind the office? Do you know someone who spends a lot of time alone at school? What might be some ways to include that person in your activities?

8 Compare and contrast Aven and Connor. Is Connor as comfortable having Tourette's as Aven is not having arms?

9 Why do Aven and Connor have a big fight? Could they have communicated their feelings to each other in a better way? How do you react when a friend hurts your feelings?

10 Aven and Connor relate to their parents very differently. What are some of those differences, and how do they influence the ways Aven and Connor see themselves?

11 What happens in chapter 34 that makes Aven feel like dancing? How might the whole story have been different if Jessica had treated Aven this way on her first day of school?

12 Think about the setting the author has chosen, Stagecoach Pass. How does it affect the way you read the story?

13 Tarantulas are important in the story. Why is their absence significant? What does Aven's search for them represent?

14 The Aven we meet at the beginning of the book is very different from the Aven at the end. How is she the same, and how has she changed? What about Connor?

15 Think of a time when you felt empathy. What can you do to be more empathetic in your daily life?

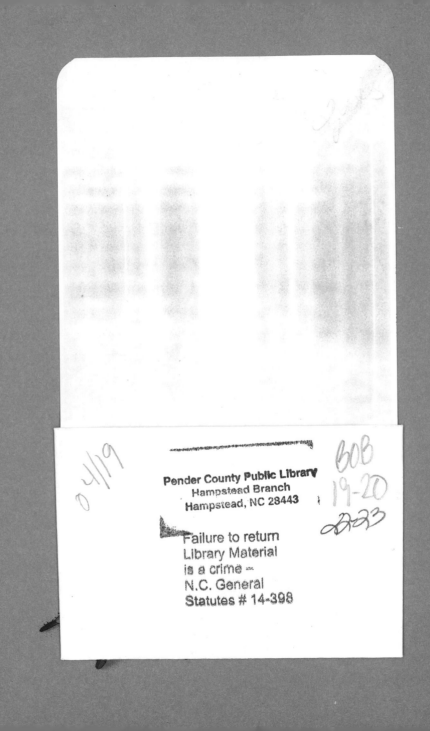